Cash Captured My Heart 2

Saved by a Boss

By. Tyanna and Jammie Jaye

Cash Captured My Heart 2: Saved by a Boss

Copyright © 2020 by Tyanna & Jammie Jaye

Published by Tyanna Presents

www.tyannapresents.1@gmail.com

This is a work of fiction. Any references or similarities to actual events, real people, living or dead, or to the real locals intended to give the novel a sense of reality. Any similarity in other names, characters, places, and incidents are entirely coincidental.

Synopsis

Love can make you do some crazy things, but heartbreak can drive you to take drastic measures...Just ask Kyndall Richardson. Not exactly hiding from love, Kyndall finds herself in an unexpected situation. One that will leave her second guessing just how good her life really was.

Shawnee's finally found the man she considered to be "the one." She's happier than she's ever been and feels that Luke was the missing piece of the puzzle that she called life. With him by her side, she has everything she's ever wanted and feels complete; nothing can steal her joy. That is until Luke's baby mama, Meia, stepped in on a mission to destroy their happily ever after.

All Cash ever wanted was to spend the rest of his life with Nadia, the woman he considered to be the love of his life. However, Nadia does the worst thing imaginable by betraying him. When Cash pulls away from Nadia, she refuses to let him go despite her lack of loyalty. She's after his heart and will stop at nothing to get it.

Will Love take Kyndall on a roller coaster ride she can't handle? Will Shawnee and Luke be able to withstand the storm known as Meia? Who will end up with Cash's heart? Continue to follow the crew in this second installment of Cash Captured My Heart: Saved by a Boss to find out what happens....

Previously in Part 1

Chrissy

Keem gotta be out of his mind if he thought I was going home. I want to see this shit play out.

He pulled out so fast that he didn't even wait to see if I was going to go the other way, which was good for me. I waited until he pulled off, then followed behind him. He was driving like a bat out of hell. I was glad that I knew where I was going because otherwise, I would have lost him.

Just as I was getting on the e-way, my phone rang. When I saw that it was my brother. I hit ignore because I knew what he wanted. As soon as I was going to power my phone off, it rang again, and I mistakenly answered it.

"Bitch, I know you saw me calling you. Why the fuck did you tell my wife that bullshit?" his voice roared through my car.

"I bet you will think twice the next time you try me. I know that you value her just like I value Keem. Now, either you can stop framing him, or I can send all of these pictures that I got of you and yo' side bitch. It's your choice, so I advise you to choose lightly," I told him.

See, he had always looked at me as if I were weak. My entire life he had run over me, but that was all over now. This was going to be the last time he did that shit to me. I couldn't understand for the life of me why he couldn't just get his own money. My brother had a degree, but he was too lazy to just grind like others do.

"How could you do that shit to me? Tara is my wife, not some bitch I was fucking. You assisted in breaking her heart, Chrissy. What have you turned in to? You are not my sister! She would never do that."

I could hear the hurt in his voice.

I felt bad because I knew that I had fucked up with the one person who had always had my best interest in mind.

"I love you, Dre, but I want my baby to grow up better than we did. He may not be with me, but trust me, we will get far more money out of him this way. I know for sure that this is his baby. So, he will have no choice," I explained.

He was quiet, so I knew he was thinking about what I had said.

"You need to fucking make this shit right with Tara. I can't lose her, Chrissy."

He sounded like he was going to cry and that alone killed me.

I was getting ready to reply, but I realized he had hung up on me. I was pulling into the park, so that was fine. I would just call him when I get done busting up this family reunion.

Cash

"Cash, where do we go from here? We can't keep sneaking around," Kyndall told me as we sat on the top of my car.

It was getting dark, so the sky was beautiful.

"I don't know. You could just move in with me," I joked.

I knew that wasn't going to happen, but I was taking my shot. I knew she cared about Keem.

"I'm not finna play with you, Cash. Just give me some time, and I will figure it out," she said as she kissed me.

This shit was life. I had to have her, and I was going to do whatever it took to make her mine.

"Have you told Shawnee about us?" I asked.

I knew that Luke knew. I was also sure that she hadn't told Shawnee. I knew she was going to be mad that we didn't tell her. She had been rooting for us for years.

"Hell no, I will never hear the end of that. Her ass blows shit out of proportion. She will be ready to tell the whole world."

She wasn't lying. Shawnee's ass had a big mouth when it came to everybody's business but hers. I knew she meant well, though. She was all about Kyndall being happy, and that was all that mattered to me. I loved the relationship they had. It was like me and Luke's friendship.

"I love you, Kyndall."

"I love you, too, Cashmere."

She kissed me, and my dick got hard instantly. That was until I heard the last voice I wanted to hear.

"Damn, so Naida wasn't lying. Yall really are fucking," Keem said as he walked up to my car.

I knew he was going to try and act tough. I just laughed. We all knew his soft ass wasn't about that life. He knew I could beat his ass with my eyes closed.

"Keem, I can explain."

I didn't know why she was trying to explain to his ass. He was the one who was around here, fucking other bitches and getting them pregnant. Not to mention, I still owed his ass for stealing from me. He had better tread lightly.

"You don't get to explain shit to him. Truth be told, he needs to be explaining some shit to you."

I knew I shouldn't have said that, but she needed to know that she was married to a bitch-ass nigga.

"What does that mean?" she asked, looking from me to Keem.

"That I'm giving him something you couldn't," Chrissy said, walking up to where we were.

I looked over at Kyndall, and I saw that look on her face again.

"Stop, just fucking stop! Cash, did you know this?"

She had tears rolling down her face.

I didn't want to answer her because I knew it would hurt her.

I dropped my head. I couldn't look at her. It made me regret not telling her when she first woke up. I just wasn't that type of nigga. I wanted him to be the one who told her.

"Yep, he knew," Chrissy blurted.

I wanted to beat her ass.

"I didn't ask you anything. Why did you even come here? What type of woman wants to see another woman hurt like this? And, Keem, I knew you had fucked someone, but I would have never thought it was her. Chrissy, you looked in my face and spoke to me the other day, knowing you were fucking my husband."

"Bitch, please! You shouldn't be mad anyway. You were just fucking another nigga. Shit, his best friend at that. And, trust me, I wasn't the only one fucking him. Isn't that right, baby daddy? Tell her who else you fucking," Chrissy said while looking at me.

This bitch was crazy.

Who does shit like this?

This was one of the reasons I didn't cheat. Side bitches didn't know their damn place.

"Chrissy, I told you to go home. Why did you come here?" Keem asked.

I wondered the same thing. What she didn't know was that she was just making shit harder on herself. If he was already avoiding her, he really wasn't going to fuck with her after this shit.

I wanted to knock her ass out, but my hand was throbbing. I knew my next stop was going to be the hospital. I didn't go last night because Kyndall had wrapped it up well. Even though she had done a good job, it was bleeding now. I guessed when I was trying to grip her waist, I hit it. I was so into her, I didn't think about my hand.

"Who else are you fucking, Keem?" Kyndall asked.

He was quiet as hell. I knew he wasn't fucking Shawnee because she damn near hated that nigga. My question was, who the hell mattered that much that she was making it their business for Kyndall to find out?

"You can tell them, or I will. Better yet, let's not waste any more time. Let's just put it all on the table. Keem, tell yo' best friend how you been fucking his girl for the past few months."

As soon as the words left her mouth, I pulled my gun out. I blacked out. I couldn't believe what the fuck I had just heard. There was no way she was telling the truth. I knew Kyndall and I were wrong, but damn, that nigga had been fucking my bitch and stealing from me.

Without looking, I let off three shots.

When I turned around, I could have died at the sight in front of me. I knew from that moment, my life would never be the same.

Chapter 1

Kyndall

I woke up in the hospital, and my head was banging. I couldn't believe Cash had shot me. That shit had fucked me up. I knew he hadn't tried to, but it happened, and that was something he couldn't take back. My heart was broken. Everything in me wanted to go back into depression mode, but I wouldn't allow it. I knew what needed to be done.

I had been waiting for the doctor to come for nearly an hour. I was getting sleepy, but I didn't want to sleep. I knew that sounded weird, but that was how I felt.

My phone was in my purse, going off. I knew it was probably Shawnee, but I didn't want to talk. I had already told the nurse to tell Cash I didn't want to be bothered. If I knew him, then he probably clicked out, but I didn't care. I was done with both him and Hakeem. They had both shown me that I meant nothing to them. How could Cash know that Keem had someone pregnant and not tell me? I would never do that to him. Let's not even talk about Keem; he was so disrespectful. He was fucking Nadia. I knew that nasty bitch didn't like me for some reason. Hell, now I knew why.

I knew I was wrong for what I had done, but he didn't catch me doing anything but kissing Cash. I loved Cash, and that was all wrong. I shouldn't have let things go as far as they did, but it was done, and I couldn't take it back.

As I laid there, I thought about the past year of my life and tears came to my eyes. I would have never thought this would be my life.

The doctors finally came in and told me I was good and that they would be letting me go home. That was when it hit me; I no longer had a home. I was ruined.

After they left out the room, I pulled my phone out and called the one person I knew would help me.

"Hey, hunny bun. I haven't heard from yo' ass in a few months," Danni answered.

"Look, girl, so much has happened. I was calling to tell you I was coming down to visit for a while."

She didn't say anything, so I knew she was thinking.

"OK, when?"

I could tell she wanted to ask me what was going on, but she didn't, and I was thankful for that.

"I will be there in the morning."

"OK… I will see you when you get here. What time does your flight land?"

"I'm getting ready to book it now. I'm on the next thing going out so I will text and let you know," I assured her.

I was happy she didn't start questioning me like she would normally do.

As soon as we ended the call, I opened my American Airlines app and booked a flight. All I was waiting for at that point were my discharge papers.

As I laid in bed, all I could think about was Cash. It hadn't even been an entire day, and I missed the hell out of him. I wanted him to be here with me so bad, but I knew that could never happen now. This shit was making me rethink my entire damn life. *Did I marry the wrong man? How long had he felt this way about me? Hell, how long did I ignore the feelings I had for him?* I had so many questions, and no one could answer them for me.

They brought my paperwork in an hour later, and I headed home so I could pack a bag. Whatever I didn't have, I would get in Memphis. I didn't take anything that could lead Cash to me. I even planned to get rid of my phone.

On the way to the airport, I stopped and got a prepaid phone, so I would be able to get in touch with Danni. I texted her from the new phone and disposed of my old one. I just wanted to be free from my life in Jersey. I planned to call Shawnee, just not today. I knew she would tell Cash where I was, and I couldn't have that.

A part of me felt that what I was doing was wrong because I was still married to Hakeem, but on the other hand, he didn't really worry when I was in a coma, or when I was gone the last time, so maybe he wouldn't this time, either. Now, he and Chrissy could be happy and raise their child.

I made a mental note to file for a divorce as soon as I got settled.

The plane ride was smooth, and a little faster than I thought it would be. As soon as I landed, I called Danni to see if she was outside. Once she confirmed she was, I grabbed my bags and headed out the door.

For some reason, as soon as I laid eyes on Danni, the tears started rolling.

She ran to me and hugged me tightly.

"Stop crying, boo. Whatever it is, it will be OK," she assured me as she ushered me to the car.

I had to stop and do a double take. My girl was riding in a fucking Bentley. The last time I had come here, she was riding in a Honda.

"Don't look like that, bitch. You've been MIA for almost four months."

As soon as the words left her mouth, I thought about my baby girl. She would have been five months. I got sad all over again.

After we were both in the car, we headed to her house.

"Bitch, where the hell are you taking me?" I asked as I watched her pass the exit we normally got off on when I would visit.

"Oh, I got a new house, too."

She smiled big as hell.

We rode for another twenty minutes before we pulled up to a large gate. When we pulled in, I was in awe. My house was nice, but my girl was living the life.

"Bitch, this is a bad house."

"Thanks."

I knew she was doing well, but I didn't know it was this good.

"Girl, who lives here in this big-ass house with you?" I asked as we walked to the door.

When we got in the foyer, I took it all in. The marble floor was to die for, and let's not talk about the huge double staircases.

"Just me, girl. I wish I had a man or kids to share it with, so it's just me and you, girl. Let me show you to your room."

I followed her as I looked at all the beautiful paintings on the walls. My girl was doing well. She deserved it, though. She had gone through something similar with her husband. The only good part was, he was killed in a head-on collision before she had a chance to divorce him. Lucky her.

"Go ahead and get a shower and meet me in the kitchen for dinner in an hour."

I nodded and made my way around the huge room, then I headed to the bathroom. It was just as big as the damn bedroom. I knew I was going to love living here.

After I showered, I headed down to eat. She had the entire house smelling good. My stomach rumbled as I walked down the stairs. This girl had a full layout like there were ten people here. I just laughed because she was being extra as hell.

"Did you really have to cook all this damn food?" I asked.

She was smiling until she saw my shoulder. Earlier, she hadn't seen it because I had a jacket on.

"What the hell happened to you, Kyndall?"

I took a deep breath before telling her what had gone down. She sat there in a daze. I knew she had a million questions she wanted to ask.

"So, where is Keem now?"

"Hell, I don't know. His ass could be dead for all I care. I'm so done with his ass. Every time I think about him, I get mad all over again. Like, how could he do me like that? I loved him with everything in me. Maybe I just wasn't enough for him. I just hope it was all worth it for him."

"Well, what about Cash? He was there for you when no one was, so you can't just say fuck him. That wouldn't be fair."

"He knew Keem was cheating and he didn't tell me or try to warn me. That was not cool at all. If I knew Nadia was fucking Keem, I would have told him right away," I fussed.

"Be for real, Kyn. That man didn't know Keem was fucking Nadia's hoe ass. Now, I will say that he should have told you about Chrissy, but he was protecting your feelings. Not only that, but you have to consider the fact that Keem was his best friend," she explained.

I knew what she was saying was true, but nothing was going to make me feel different. He should have told me, and that was that.

"Well, I think you should call him and at least hear him out. And how long do you plan on hiding out here? Not that I care; I just want to know. Hell, I'm happy to have some company."

I just shook my head.

She was so damn extra. Her ass was still ghetto as hell. I guess that would never change.

We talked all damn night. I think it was after five when we fell asleep on the couch. It felt good to talk to someone about how I really felt.

Cash

I had been sitting in the damn waiting room for hours, and no one was telling me anything about Kyndall. I knew she had probably told them not to tell me. I really hadn't tried to shoot her. I would never do that.

I paid the receptionist to go and check on Kyndall, so I was just waiting for her to come back.

"Hey, she's been discharged," the nurse said as she sat back at her desk.

I just shook my head. I knew she was going to pull something like this.

When I made it to my car, I called her phone but didn't get an answer. I knew she needed some space, so I would just call her tomorrow. I needed to go and find this Nadia hoe. I was going to make her regret the day she met me.

She thought I didn't know that she still had her house, but she was mistaken. I knew everything.

I hopped on the expressway and headed to her house. I called Luke so he could meet me. I hadn't really told them what happened because I knew Shawnee was going to try and kill my ass. I would just let Kyndall tell them. I did tell them that I had shot Keem's bitch ass.

After he confirmed he would meet me, I called the cleanup crew so they would be on standby. If she was here, then she was going to die a slow death. I didn't give a damn about her being pregnant. Hell, the baby probably wasn't mine anyway.

When I pulled up to her house, I smiled because she was home. I wanted this to be fast, so I called Luke. He said he was pulling up on the next street, so I headed to the door. I knew she was going to be happy to see me because I hadn't been answering for her.

KNOCK! KNOCK!

She swung the door open without even asking who it was. She had the biggest smile on her face, but that wouldn't be there long.

"Hey, baby."

"What's good?" I greeted, walking past her.

"Nothing. I've been calling you, baby. We missed you," she lied, rubbing her belly.

I smiled because she had really tried to play me. I couldn't believe I had put this lying bitch before Kyndall. Just thinking about that shit made me madder by the second.

"So, what's up? You got something you wanna tell me?" I asked, standing against the wall.

Now she looked like she was sad. I kind of wondered whether she knew what I was asking. Shit, there was no telling how much shady shit she had been doing.

"Nah, baby, what you talking about?"

I laughed because she was really playing this role. Damn, I was rethinking so much shit. So, if she was fucking Keem, who was that nigga, Dre? I knew it wasn't my homeboy. That would mean I would have to kill him, too.

"Cash!" she yelled, pulling me from my thoughts.

Just as I was getting ready to talk, I heard something fall in the back of the house.

I grabbed her and pulled her with me. I knew Luke would be here in a second, so I wasn't worried about whoever it was.

"Before we walk in this room, I'm going to ask you something. Please don't lie to me, Nadia," I urged.

She was going to die either way, but I wanted to know what I was up against, especially since the door was closed. She didn't say anything, so I knew there was a nigga in there. Whoever he was, I hope he said his prayers, because today was his last day walking on this green earth.

I knocked the door open and got the shock of my life.

"You gotta be kidding me. Damn, you were fucking my best friend and a nigga who worked for me? Which one of them yo' baby daddy?" I asked.

She looked like a deer caught in headlights.

"Aw, you didn't think I knew about that, huh? Well, I do. I just hope he was worth you losing your life."

"What the fuck this nigga doing here?" Luke asked as he came into the room.

I looked at him and smiled. He knew what that meant. He sent a bullet through his forehead. That was why he was my nigga. I didn't have to tell him shit because he already knew.

I threw Nadia to the floor and she sobbed like that shit would change something.

"Please don't kill me," she begged.

"Luke, do you hear this shit?" I joked.

She had lost her fucking mind if she thought I wouldn't kill her. That was a dead subject. She was as good as dead the moment she fucked my best friend.

"Look, man, I know you wanna kill her, but what if the baby is yours?" Luke asked.

I really didn't give a damn about the baby at the moment because I was so in my feelings.

I stood for a minute, looking down at her with so much hatred in my eyes. I couldn't stand the sight of her at the moment.

"Luke, get that bitch the fuck out of my face. Take her to the spot and get some around-the-clock security. She is not to go out anywhere. Doctors are to come to her. Make sure Mrs. Lucille is free to stay at the crib with her. Tell her I'll triple her pay."

Mrs. Lucille was my maid. She was an older lady who used to babysit me when I was younger. When I got older, she started a cleaning business, and I hired her to clean all my stores and houses. Well, now that her business was booming from the contract she had gotten with me, she was usually vacationing. So, since she was going to be watching this hoe for me, it was only right that I made it worth her time.

Luke dialed the cleanup crew, then hung up, and that was their cue to come.

I looked down at Nadia in disgust. I really cared about her. Hell, I even loved her, but not like I loved Kyndall. Just thinking about all the hurt she had helped cause Kyndall made me want to say fuck that baby and kill her.

I walked out because I still wanted to empty my clip into her stupid ass.

Shawnee

"Nee-Nee, do I have to go with my mommy?"

I knew that question was coming. For some reason, Joi hated going with Meia. It almost made me think she was doing something to her. I wanted to ask her what was going on, but I was almost afraid of what she would tell me. I knew Luke would flip if I told him how she acted every time it was time for her to go to her mom's house.

"Well, baby, I can call your daddy, and we can see what he says."

I knew what his answer was going to be, but I couldn't make any decision without him. If it were up to me, she would never go over there. The last time she went, she came back looking a mess, and that shit pissed me off.

I decided I would just call Luke while she wasn't around so I could tell him what I thought was going on.

"OK, baby, go to your room and play. I will call Daddy."

As soon as she was in her room, I called him. He told me he was pulling up, so I headed to the kitchen so I could start cooking. He had been out all day, so I knew he would be hungry.

While in the kitchen alone, I took a moment to look back on the past few months of my life, and things had changed so much. I would have never thought I would love someone so much. Let's not talk about Joi. I never really wanted kids because I thought I would be a bad mother like my mom was. Joi had shown me that I was capable of being a good mother. I guess it was more so me trying to prove to myself that I could do better.

"Hey, baby," Luke greeted me as he came into the kitchen.

I looked at him and couldn't do anything but smile. My man was the shit.

"Hey, I wanted to talk to you about Joi and her going over to Meia's house. There has to be something going on over there. The last time I went to drop her off, she cried the whole way there, then she just came in here and said she didn't want to go. I think we need to keep her at home for a while."

"Why haven't you told me this, baby? I wouldn't have been sending her over there. Shit, if she doesn't want to go, then she doesn't have to go. Did you ask what was going on over there that made her not want to go?"

"No."

He just nodded and headed out the kitchen. He came back with Joi.

I admired how he was with her. I wished my father would have been like that. He put Joi's needs before anything, and that was all that mattered to him.

"So, tell Daddy and Nee-Nee what happens when you're at your mom's house."

She looked at me like she was getting the OK to answer him. I could tell he noticed because he smiled.

"Um, she always tells me that I have to go to my room and she gets mad when I say that I'm hungry. And the other day, when I said Nee-Nee makes me cookies, she hit me, and she says my granny is a bad word. And that man told her not to answer for you so you can give her money to get me back, but Nee-Nee came and got me."

Luke's face was so red. I knew he was going to kill Meia. I kind of felt bad for Joi because she didn't know what she had just told her dad would end her mother's life.

She told us a few other things, then Luke left the room. I knew he was going to get his mind in order, so I kept Joi in the kitchen. I knew she would want to help me cook. That little girl loved cooking.

After dinner was done, I sent Joi to wash up, and I headed to tell Luke that it was time to eat.

He was sitting in his office in the dark.

"Hey, baby. I need you to get it together so we can have dinner. I know you will handle her, but we can worry about that later. Joi is right here with us. She won't be able to hurt her anymore," I told him.

He kissed me with so much passion, my panties were now wet.

"Thank you, baby," was all he said before walking out the door.

I followed him, and we headed to eat dinner. When I walked into the kitchen, they were both sitting at the table talking. I just smiled and fixed our food.

After we were done eating, Luke looked lost.

"Baby, what you think about this?" I asked. He gave me a sad look that I couldn't read.

"Look, I have to tell you something, but you have to give me your gun first."

He had lost his damn mind if he thought I was going to do that. Him saying that only told me that I was going to want to kill someone, and that wasn't good.

"Spill it."

"Have you talked to Kyn?" he asked, beating around the bush.

"Luke, get to the point."

"So, Keem caught Kyndall and Cash together and a lot of other shit popped off. Keem and Kyn got shot."

I knew he was leaving something out, and I could tell what he was leaving out played a big part in what he was trying to tell me.

I pulled out my phone and called Cash.

"What's good, sis?" he answered.

"I need you to come to the house."

He assured me he was coming, and I took Luke's phone because I knew he would text him.

I grabbed a bottle of wine and sat on the couch. I knew Cash had shot my cousin, but I wanted to hear him say it. I called Luke's mother and had her come get Joi because I knew shit was about to get ugly.

After a full bottle of wine and three cookies, Cash's ass walked through the door, looking crazy.

Luke thought my gun was upstairs, but it was in my purse the whole time. He did his best to try and keep me downstairs. I just laughed because neither of them had any idea what kind of beast they had unleashed. It was worse because Kyndall wasn't answering her phone.

"So, Cash, where is Kyndall?"

He gave me this weird look, so I knew he didn't know.

"I don't know."

I sat up on the couch so I could make sure I heard him right.

"So, you're telling me you don't know where my cousin is?"

He stood there, looking at me crazy, but that was cool. I already had my gun out, and neither of them had a clue.

"So, tell me what happened?"

Maybe he would know the answer to that.

"We met at the park because she said she needed to talk, and the next thing I knew, Keem was pulling up."

"So, that's all?" I questioned.

Both he and Luke just sat there and looked at me like I was crazy, and that shit pissed me off.

"OK, so let me ask you this. Did. You. Shoot. My. Cousin?"

He gave me a sad look that answered my question, so I pulled out my gun and shot his ass in the foot. I knew he would be mad at me, but I didn't care.

"Yo, Shawnee, what the fuck?" he yelled as he fell to the floor.

Luke walked over and really thought he was going to take my shit.

"Unless you wanna be down there with him, I would advise you to get away from me," I said, pointing my gun towards his foot.

If for a second Cash thought he was going to get away with shooting my cousin, he was fooled.

"Now, you need to get out of my house and don't talk to me until you find her."

As soon as they were gone, I headed to my room. I laid on the bed and cried my heart out. I felt so bad for Kyndall because shit just wasn't getting better for her. It seemed that no matter how much she wanted things to go right, they just didn't. I wished she would just answer for me. I just wanted to hear her voice.

Chapter 2

Chrissy

It had been almost a week since Keem had been shot, and I had been here every day since it had happened. I just prayed he would wake up. I also prayed Kyndall was dead. That way, I could have him to myself. I knew he was going to be mad at me, but that was OK because after he heard that his wife hadn't been up here to check on him, all of that would change.

I loved Hakeem more than he knew. I just wished he could see that. Hell, I loved his ass more than I loved myself. Since I knew his nurse wouldn't be back for at least an hour, I headed to shower. I hated the shower here. I wanted to go home and shower, but I wanted to be here when he woke up, or just in case she tried to come.

I knew I couldn't keep her from coming up here, but I knew that if she saw me, she would leave. I couldn't lie and say that I wasn't jealous of her because I was. She had two fine-ass men following behind her, and she was drop-dead gorgeous. The only thing I had on her was the fact that I was going to give Keem a baby. I knew how bad he wanted a baby, so I had made sure I got pregnant.

I had been taking Geritol for the last six months. I had even gone as far as poking holes in the condoms that were in his desk drawer, but I guess God was looking out for me because he hadn't used one since the first time we fucked.

After I showered, I headed back in the room and saw that I had like ten missed calls from my sister-in-law. I put my things away and called her back.

"Hey, you called?"

"Yea, just wanted to see if you talked to Dre. He hasn't called or been home in nearly a week. I know he's mad at me, but that's not like him," she finished.

I knew what had probably happened, but there was no way I was going to tell her that unless I knew for sure.

"I will try calling him, and I will call you back."

I ended the call and paced the floor.

I knew I couldn't make any moves without talking to Keem, and his ass was in a fucking coma.

I picked up my phone and called Dre's best friend.

"Hey, I was calling to see if you've heard from Dre?" I asked.

"Naw, it's been about a week."

I sighed because that was my confirmation.

He flirted with me like always, then I ended the call.

I needed to figure out something fast. I wanted to call my sister-in-law back, but I didn't because she was going to start asking questions I didn't have the answers to. All I could do was cry because I was the one who had pulled him into this shit. Not only had I pulled him into this, but I was the reason Cash had gone crazy. All I wanted was for Keem to love our baby and me. I didn't mean for all of this to get out of hand.

Now I'd lost my brother, the only person who had ever loved me.

I curled up on the couch in the hospital room and watched Keem lay there with all those tubes hooked up to him. He had to survive; I had nobody but him and my baby.

****

The sounds of the machines beeping and Keem knocking shit around woke me up out of my sleep.

I ran over to his side, trying to calm him down.

The doctors and nurses ran into the room.

"Calm down, Mr. Richardson, or we will have to give you something to calm you," the doctor said while pinning him down.

Keem calmed down a little, but he was trying to pull the tube out of his throat. The doctor put gloves on and told the nurse to get him a cup of water. Once they had everything in place, they took the tube out and gave Keem a sip of water.

His voice was a little raspy, and they couldn't really hear what he said, so the nurse gave him a notepad and a pen. He scribbled on the paper, asking for his wife.

My heart broke instantly. He didn't even ask whether I was OK after he had been swinging like crazy. I didn't even feel like being there at the moment, so I decided to go down to the hospital cafeteria.

While I was down there, I called Dre's best friend, Keys so he could come join me. I didn't have anyone else to talk to, and I needed to vent.

After sitting in the cafeteria for a half hour, in my thoughts, Keys finally walked in.

"What's good, little mama?"

I didn't know what it was, but as soon as I saw him, the tears started to fall.

"My life is a complete mess. I'm about to be someone's mother, and I don't even have my shit together."

"What's wrong? Why are you crying?" he asked while wiping my face.

Keys had always liked me, but I would never give him the time of day. I felt like he wasn't for me because he wasn't rolling in the dough. Then, one night we all got drunk, and we ended up sleeping together. We kept it a secret so Dre wouldn't know.

To be honest with y'all, that night, I believe I got pregnant with this baby, so yeah, there was a chance of it being Keys' baby. Not to mention that when I first told Keem I was pregnant, I wasn't. So, Keem and Kyndall thought I was four months pregnant, but I had just barely made three.

"I'm just going through so much right now and don't know what to do."

"First of all, stop crying and let's get you something to eat. You can't be all stressed out like this while you're carrying my baby."

"Keys, this is not your baby, so why do you keep saying that?"

Every time Keys saw me, he said that, but I kept telling him it wasn't, although, there was a strong possibility it was. I wouldn't tell him that, though. That was probably the reason I'd never been to the doctor: I was scared to find out the truth.

"Because I know it's mine, but we will wait to see when it gets here. I'm sure it's going to look just like me."

Ignoring his ass, I picked up the menu and tried to figure out what I wanted to eat.

"So, have you heard from my brother yet?"

"No, and the shit isn't looking good. When was the last time you heard from him?"

"About a week ago. I know something probably happened to him because he was always into some shit," I assured Keys.

He looked at me with a raised eyebrow, and I knew he wanted to ask questions.

"What you mean, he was always into something? Dre didn't hide shit from me, so what was he doing that you know about, and I don't?"

I wasn't going there with Keys. I did not need anything happening to his crazy ass when he was all I had left besides Keem.

"Nothing, now can we please get something to eat and talk about something different?"

We sat, talked and ate lunch.

When he left, I headed back upstairs with Keem. Hopefully, he was in a better mood.

Keem

When I woke up, I was in a strange place with tubes and shit hooked up to me. The last thing I remembered was my wife and I being shot. I needed to know where she was because I didn't see her face. All I saw was Chrissy's sorry ass, and I wasn't beat for seeing her. Not seeing Kyndall made me think the worst.

I started writing on the paper, asking a bunch of questions, and Chrissy's stupid ass left the room, knowing she was the only one who knew what had happened after we were shot.

After the doctors explained to me what had happened, I thought to myself, *I'm lucky to be alive.* He told me the bullet hit me in my chest, and my right lung collapsed, so they needed to insert a chest tube to drain the blood so I could breathe better. Then, they put me in a medically-induced coma so my body could rest. After he assured me that I needed to stay here for a couple more days and gave me some pain medicine, he headed out.

I laid there, looking out the window, wondering why the hell I had let my life get so out of control.

"Hey, baby, are you OK?"

"Chrissy, where is my wife?"

"I don't know. I haven't seen her since that night."

"Did she survive? Is she here at this hospital?" I snapped.

It just didn't seem realistic that she didn't know anything. She wasn't shot, so she had to see what had gone down after Cash lost it.

"Keem, I don't know. After you were shot, Cash picked Kyndall up and left me and you there, so I called the ambulance and told them there was a drive-by while we were in the park. Detectives came while you were in a coma, and I told them the same thing."

I was furious, so I decided not to say anything else to her until I cooled down.

The tap on my door brought me out of my thoughts. I didn't feel like any company, so I didn't answer.

Instead, Chrissy got up and answered the door. Shawnee came storming in, pushed Chrissy out of the way and headed to my bed.

"Where the fuck is my cousin, Keem? You sitting in here with your new family while she is missing. I'ma tell you like I told Cash, if one of y'all don't find her, I'ma kill somebody."

"Well, how is he supposed to go look for her? Don't you see what shape he is in?"

Shawnee turned to her as if she had two heads. I knew shit was about to get ugly because Shawnee was no joke.

"Listen, Suzy Homewrecker, don't talk to me. You don't know me. Just because you got the dick, don't mean shit. Facts remain the same! He's my cousin's husband, and she can come in here and tell them she doesn't want you here, so don't talk shit like you the wife, bitch. You better let her know she doesn't want these problems, Keem. I'll beat that bastard child right out her fucking stomach."

Chrissy was about to say something until I cut her off.

"Chrissy, go get me something to drink."

She knew what it was. She sucked her teeth, then headed out the door.

"Shawnee, I don't know where Kyndall is. I just woke up from an induced coma. When I woke up, Kyn was the first person I looked for, but I didn't see her."

"What the fuck happened at that park, Keem?"

"I caught her with Cash at the park. Right before I was about to go the fuck off, Chrissy aired out all my dirty laundry, which caused Cash to snap."

"Why did you ruin my cousin's life, Keem? She did nothing but love you."

"Yeah, whatever, Shawnee. She didn't love me. She loved Cash, so save that love shit. We both did some fucked-up shit in this relationship, so y'all can stop blaming me."

"Nigga, go on ahead with that dumb shit 'cause if you were the man she needed you to be, Cash wouldn't have even made it as far as he did with her. He stepped up on his grown man shit, which was something her husband should have been doing. Since you have a new family, when I find my cousin, I'll tell her you're happy," Shawnee said while headed for the door.

As soon as she opened it, Chrissy came in.

"Yeah, you're happy as shit right now, thinking you got ya man, but hunny, always remember you lose them how you get them. Now let that shit marinate in that small-ass brain of yours," Shawnee said while bursting out laughing.

Chrissy came over to me and sat juice on the table. She was about to go sit down, but I told her to sit on the bed next to me. At first, she hesitated, but she eventually sat down.

I grabbed her hand and held it tight before I spoke.

"You know if it weren't for you, all of this wouldn't have gone down. If I find out you know anything about where my wife is, and you're not telling me, I will take my baby and move far away, and you will never see it. Don't fuck with me, Chrissy, because I'm not the one to be fucked with."

After I squeezed the shit out of her hand, she got up, walked over to the couch and sat down.

The pain was starting to take over my body, so I calmed down and tried to take a nap.

Chapter three

Luke

It had been an entire week, and I hadn't heard from Cash. I'd been handling him and Keem's part of the business, not to mention, I had to find a new dude to take Dre's spot. I had also sent money to his wife for her and his kids. I didn't even know that nigga had kids. Cash would have said fuck that nigga, but when it comes to the wife, kids, and mother, I couldn't see myself not giving up something. I knew Cash was going through something, so that was why I was letting him chill. I'd even been checking on Nadia and Ms. Lucille. At first, Nadia wasn't eating, so I had to go over there and threaten her stupid ass. She needed to feed that baby in case it was my godchild.

My phone rang, bringing me out of my thoughts.

"What's good? Who's this?"

"Now, is that the way you answer the phone?" Cash's mama fussed.

"My fault, Mama Della. I didn't look to see who was calling. What can I do for you?"

"Have you seen Cash? I've been calling him for days."

This nigga hasn't even been calling his mama? Yeah, he's fucked up right now.

"I actually haven't talked to him, but I'm on my way over there now, so when I get with him, I'll call you back."

"OK, baby. Carson and I are having Sunday dinner, so come on over and bring ya mom and my little Joi."

"All right, Mama Della. I'll be over, and can I bring my girl with me?"

"Sure, baby. She must be someone important if you want to bring her to a family dinner."

"Yeah, she is, that's why I want you to meet her."

We talked a little longer, then I started my car and headed straight to Cash's crib. His ass needed to get it together, and fast.

After about twenty minutes, I pulled up to Cash's crib. His car was here, and another car was behind it, so I knew he was here.

Once I parked, I hopped out, walked up to the front door and started banging on it. I didn't get an answer, so I tried the back door.

Why the hell is this shit unlocked? This nigga has lost his damn mind.

When I walked in, there were Chinese food containers, pizza boxes, and liquor bottles everywhere. Yeah, my boy wasn't in his right state of mind.

He didn't even eat Chinese food or drink like that.

Since he wasn't in the living room, I made my way up to his bedroom. There he was, stretched out on the bed, along with two chicks.

I stood in the doorway and shook my head at his crazy ass.

I walked over to the bed and snatched one of the hoes up.

"Yo, homegirl, wake ya friend up and get the fuck out!" I barked.

"You don't have to be so rude. Who are you anyway?"

"Listen, bitch, do what I said without asking all them damn questions. You got ten minutes, or I'm shooting you and your friend."

She hurried and got her ass up. She went around to the other side of the bed to wake her friend. Within ten minutes, they were both running out the door.

Cash's ass was still laying there, even with all the yelling and noise I was making. Why wasn't this nigga awake yet? I felt his pulse, and he was alive, so I guessed it was the liquor he had consumed.

I got up and walked to the bathroom to grab a cup of water. As soon as I made it back to the room, I dumped it on his ass. The way he jumped up from the bed had me cracking the hell up.

"Man, Luke, what the fuck are you doing?"

"Nigga, what the fuck were you doing in here with two hoes, dead to the world with the fucking door unlocked. Cash, you fucking up, man! They could have robbed you or set you up. I had to throw a cup of water on you to get you up. What the fuck were you drinking last night?"

"I was drinking Henny, and I popped a pill. That shit had me gone."

He said that shit as if it were normal. I just shook my head.

"So, you use your own product now? What the fuck is wrong with you, Cash?"

"Come on, Luke, I ain't trying to hear no fucking pep talk like you're my parents. I know I'm fucking up right now, but man, I'm in my feelings right now and don't know how to cope with this shit. I fucking shot Kyndall, and now she's fucking gone, Luke. She is probably never coming back, and it's all my fault. Then Shawnee's not talking to me, and she shot me. Like, that's my sis, man."

This nigga was for real crying. This big-ass thug was fucking crying.

"She'll be back, man, you just have to give her some time."

"I'm just as bad as Keem. She's not going to want me."

"I know one thing, you better get out of this bitch-ass mood you in and get ya life together, man. You need to call ya mama, too. She's been fucking calling you for days, and you didn't answer. I'ma tell you like this, if it's meant to be, she will be back, but if not, fuck it, life goes on. You can't be out here sleeping on these streets. You can lose everything you've worked hard for in a quick second because you fell off your game. Yeah, I'm here for you and got you covered, but nigga, I got my own family. It's been a whole week since I've had family time with my daughter, and a couple days since I've fucked my girl, all because I've been handling your business. I always got ya back, but this shit you got going on needs to stop today. Get the fuck up and take a shower and let's go see ya mama."

After I told his ass how I felt, he jumped up and limped his ass to the bathroom to take care of his hygiene. While he did that, I made my way downstairs and started picking up the trash that was all over his crib.

After I was finished picking up the empty food containers, I called Ms. Lucille to send some cleaners over here to give his house a good cleaning. I even told her to make sure she told them to trash his sheets and put some new ones on the bed.

The minute I was about to put my phone back in my pocket, a text came through from Shawnee.

Babe: What you doing, sexy?

Me: Sitting here waiting for Cash's bitch ass.

Babe: I've been missing you like crazy.

Me: I know, baby, I'm sorry. I've been handling business for Cash.

Babe: I know, that's why I haven't been bitching.

Me: Well, tonight, when I'm finished, how about I take my favorite girl out.

Babe: I think I'll love that.

Me: Be ready at eight.

I looked at my watch. I saw it was five, so I had plenty of time to roll out with Cash.

"Are you ready to go?" Cash asked while walking into the living room.

This nigga had really just thrown on something. He was wearing black Nike joggers, a green, blue and yellow YSL shirt and gold and white Jordan 11s. I wanted to say something, but I decided against it. If he wanted to look like a fool, then that was on him.

"Yeah, and I called Ms. Lucille to send someone over to clean up."

"OK, cool, thanks, man."

"You're welcome. Now, come on, let's go see Mama Della before she sends the police looking for you. If you don't answer anyone else, nigga, answer your mama. You can't be having her scared."

"I know, man, and I'll apologize to my mama when I get there."

I looked at him and shook my head. This nigga looked like shit. He needed his dreads twisted and a lineup. He was really letting his shit go over Kyndall's ass.

Shawnee

I walked around my closet, looking for something to wear. It had been a while since my baby and I had spent time together. Joi was at his mom's house for the weekend, so we had plenty of time.

I cut on Pandora, and Yo Gotti blasted from the speakers, and that was when it hit me. I picked up my phone and scrolled to my girl Danni's number.

"Hey, boo," she answered, all happy and shit.

"Hey, chica, put that bitch Kyndall on this phone. I know she's there because there ain't but two people she trusts other than Mom-Mom Ella and me, and that's you and Cash's bitch ass."

She was laughing so hard, I couldn't be serious. I had to laugh.

"Girl, what you talking about?"

I didn't reply, I just hit the FaceTime button. I knew Kyndall's ass was there. There was nowhere else she could be. Kyndall was anti-social. She didn't do the whole new people thing.

When she picked up, she turned the phone, and there my baby was, laying on the couch, asleep.

"I just wanted to make sure she was OK. How is she?"

I knew she probably wasn't well, but I was happy to lay eyes on her.

"She's taking it one day at a time. She just thinks life will never get better for her. Honestly, I think she is OK with the betrayal from Keem, but Cash is a whole different story. She made me take down all the pictures of Cash and us from our school days. My wall around her is bare as hell. Hell, I'm just mad that she didn't listen years ago when we told her that Hakeem wasn't shit."

"I know, girl. I have to come down so you can meet my new boo once all of this is over. Don't tell her you talked to me. I just needed to know she was good. Take care of her, Danni. She already thinks no one cares," I finished before we said our goodbyes and hung up.

I felt so much better knowing she was OK. I knew I wouldn't be able to tell Cash. His ass would have been on the first flight out.

It was crazy how all these years we had been telling them that they loved each other, and it took this bullshit to happen for them to see it. We had been telling them this way before she and Hakeem started dating.

Just as I hung up, my baby walked in the door, looking good enough to eat. I wanted him so bad, but we had reservations at The Chop House, and they didn't play. If you were five minutes late, they canceled your reservation, and you had to wait.

"Baby, I have your clothes laid out on the bed. Go ahead and take a shower. I will be waiting for you," I said, kissing him.

He smiled and walked off. I knew he wanted me to come and shower with him, but that wasn't going to happen.

I went to Joi's room so I could make sure everything was in place. Since he refused to let me go back to my own house, this had become my house. I wasn't complaining, either. I had a nice house, but I could set mine in his living room.

Thirty minutes later, he came down the stairs dressed in a pair of black Balmain jeans and a button-down Gucci shirt with the matching sneakers.

I could smell his YSL cologne from across the room.

"Hey, baby. You can stop staring at me. I ain't going nowhere, but in between them legs when we get back."

I blushed like a big-ass kid. That shit was crazy. I had for real butterflies. Luke was my everything. It seemed like he had come out of nowhere and showed me what real love was. I never thought I would find love like this. It was like the love you read about in books.

"Why the hell you over there smiling? What you thinking about?" he asked, pulling me from my thoughts.

"Nothing, just thinking about us and what we are building."

"Aww, let me find out you in love with a real nigga," he joked.

"Yes, I love you, baby, and I miss you. I feel like I haven't seen you all day."

"Well, you have me now, baby. And again, I'm sorry I've been away so much. Hopefully, Cash has his shit together now."

I knew Cash was going through it, and it almost made me want to forgive him since I knew where Kyndall was, but I needed to make him sweat.

"Shit, I'm just happy that nigga is up and working. I just hope Kyn is OK because I know that shit is driving him crazy. That nigga talked about her the whole damn day. I had to clean his bar out, and that shit is in the trunk of my car. He gon' drink his damn self to death."

We talked for the rest of the ride. It was the most amazing feeling. I wouldn't change it for the world.

Chapter Four

Cash

I had been looking all over for Kyndall, and she was hiding well. It had been over a month since the shooting, and I was going crazy. On top of that, Shawnee wasn't talking to me, either. I knew she knew where Kyndall was, she just didn't want to tell me. I needed to do something to get in her good graces, I just didn't know what. Shawnee was so fucking mean.

I decided to go and check on Nadia today since I hadn't seen her since the day I hid her ass from the world. I couldn't wait to blow her fucking head off. That bitch had violated me in the worst way. I would have never thought that my worker was the Dre who was texting her all the time. Here I was thinking she was fucking with one nigga, but she was fucking with two, and they were both close to me.

Technically, Dre didn't owe me any loyalty, but Keem did. That nigga and I had been kicking it since the sandbox. That shit fucked me up. Granted, I knew I fucked up by fucking his wife, but she should have been my wife anyway. He didn't deserve Kyndall.

My phone rang, pulling me from my thoughts.

"Yo?"

"Nigga, what you doing?" Luke asked as soon as I answered.

"Shit, at the office, finishing up some paperwork, then going to the warehouse so I can do a count. What you up to?"

"Shit, just picked Joi up from my mama's house. I'm about to stop at Meia's house. Joi asked for her earlier. I really don't want to go over there. I think that hoe on that dog food. Like the other day, Ben told me he saw her on the corner and shit. I really don't want Joi to see her like that."

I knew where he was coming from because I would have been the same way. I loved Joi, and I would hate to have to kill her mama for hurting her.

Luke told me a while back what Joi said, and that shit still bothered me.

"Come to the house when you are done," he told me before ending the call.

I finished up what I was doing and headed out. Since my office was all the way across the city, it took me a while to get there. The whole way, all I could think about was Kyndall. I missed her like crazy. I just wished she would call me so I could tell her how much I love her. I had looked all over this city for her, and she was nowhere to be found. I had even had my homie check to see if she had changed her number again. Each time I thought about the fact that she was gone, it made me want to kill Keem and that bitch Chrissy. She knew what she was doing. She wanted to hurt Kyndall, and I had no idea why. Kyndall hadn't done anything to her other than being married to Keem.

I pulled up to the warehouse, and there were two cars I didn't recognize. I shot Luke a text, then headed for the door.

When I walked in, two of my workers were counting, and there were two more bottling pills.

"What's good, boss man?" one of them asked.

I nodded and headed to my office. I thought about asking whose cars were outside, but I decided I would just roll the cameras back and see for myself. I didn't trust anyone, so I wanted to be sure that no fuck shit was going on.

I watched the movement going in and out of the building all day, and I didn't see anything out of line, so I closed my laptop and headed to check on my hoe ass, so-called baby mama.

I knew the ride was going to be short, so I lit a little piece of blunt I had from earlier.

I pulled in the gate, and my phone rang. It was a female I had met named Tori. I had been kicking it with her tough since Kyndall had been gone. I knew she was digging a nigga, but I didn't want to play with her feelings like that. I knew whenever Kyndall showed her face that it would be over for ol' girl. Her head game was on point, though, so that was the reason I had kept her around.

"What's good, ma?"

"Nothing, baby. I was calling to see what you were doing. I was hoping I was going to see you later."

"I can make that happen. Give me a minute to finish up some shit, then I'ma call you," I told her as I walked to the door.

We ended the call just as I walked in. Nadia was sitting on the couch, looking good as hell. The pregnancy had her glowing. *Shit,* I mumbled as I adjusted my dick. I knew fucking her would be a bad move, but damn. She looked at me with the saddest eyes, and I walked past her and went into the kitchen where Mrs. Lucille was.

"Hey, handsome. What brings you around here?" she asked as if this wasn't my house.

"I just wanted to come and check on y'all," I admitted.

"Good. Are you staying for dinner?"

"Yea, I can do that."

I went back in the living room, and Nadia was gone. I made my way to the back of the house, and all I could hear were her cries. As much as I wanted to comfort her, I knew she would make me weak, and I couldn't have that.

Although she had done some fucked-up shit, I still had love for her at one point. It wasn't like the love I had for Kyn, but it was genuine love. It took everything for me to walk back to the living room.

I took a seat in the chair, so I could see the whole room.

"All that damn girl does is cry," Mrs. Lucille said, handing me a bottle of water.

"I don't know what for. She did this to herself."

"I guess. Just go talk to her, Cashmere."

I hated to be called by my government name, and she knew that. I wouldn't dare say anything to her about it, though.

"OK." I got up and went in the room.

She was getting out the shower, and my dick sprang up as I made my way to her. No words were spoken as I pulled her closer to me. She looked like she was scared as hell.

I sat on the bed and looked at her. She was beautiful as hell. She dropped to her knees and pulled my joggers down all the way. As soon as her mouth touched my dick, I felt like I was in heaven. Her mouth was warm as hell.

"Fuck," I moaned.

I missed this shit, I couldn't lie. I didn't want to nut, so I pulled away and picked her up. She opened her legs, and I had to lick my lips. Her pussy was beautiful.

I entered her, and my knees damn near buckled. That let me know Tori's pussy was garbage as hell because nothing like this had ever happened. It could have been the fact that I kind of missed her, though.

"Damn, I miss you," I moaned as I slid in and out of her wet pussy.

"I miss you, too, baby," she moaned as she matched my strokes.

I wasn't lying when I said that. I missed her, but my mind was on Kyndall.

I closed my eyes, and all I could see was Kyndall riding my dick. Before I knew it, I was busting. After I was done, I pulled my pants up and walked to my car. There was no way I would be able to look at her.

As soon as I pulled out the driveway, Mrs. Lucille called.

"Boy, I said go and talk to her, not go and fuck the damn girl. Why would you do that dumb shit if you know there is no chance of y'all being together? That is leading her on. Although she fucked up, there is a chance she could be having your child, and all this crying is going to hurt the baby. You need to turn your ass around and come fix this shit," was all she said before hanging up on my ass.

What she said was right, but there was no way I could look Nadia in the face right now. She was just going to be mad at me.

I headed straight home. All I wanted to do was be alone. I had fucked up, and I needed to figure out how I was going to fix it. I felt like I had cheated on Kyndall. The crazy thing was, I never once felt like that when I fucked Tori.

Kyndall

"Yea, boo, you wanna go with me? I need to go look at the restaurant I'm thinking about opening," Danni asked as she walked into my room.

"Sure. It's not like I'm doing anything else," I replied, getting smart.

She was always telling me what I wasn't doing. What she didn't know was that I had been writing. I loved reading and figured I could put all this drama that was going on in my life into a book. I have been writing it for the past month.

I closed my laptop and got out of bed. I had showered a few hours ago, so I found some PINK tights and pulled them out to put on. Since I had been wearing my hair natural, I decided to just put it in a bun.

Once I made sure I looked good, I headed downstairs. Danni was sitting on the couch dressed in an outfit similar to mine. Seeing her dressed like me made me think of Shawnee. I missed her, but I was avoiding calling because I knew she was going to flip out on my ass. I was awake the day she had called Danni, I just played sleep because I didn't want to talk at the time. Now I missed her and Joi like crazy. Hell, I missed home, period. The only person I had been talking to was Mom-Mom Ella. I knew there was no way I could go without talking to her. The last time I did that shit, she told me she was going to beat the skin off me if I did it again.

"Let's roll."

 I grabbed my purse and walked out the door behind her.

When we got in the car, she hooked her phone to the Bluetooth and pulled out the driveway.

"Girl, I swear I miss my damn phone. I can't do shit on this prepaid phone. I want to go get one, but knowing Cash, he probably got a damn Amber Alert out on my ass."

"Bitch, you do know that's for kids, right?"

"Well, hell, that's what he treats me like. Hell, I'm glad he doesn't know where you live. Trust me, his ass would have been here the day I left," I told her.

She knew Cash, but not well. See, when they were around each other, he was all sweet and shit.

"I'm not finna play with you and Cash's ass. That nigga is going to find you, and when he does, he will hold yo' ass hostage."

We both laughed because that was the honest to God truth.

I was getting ready to reply and got light headed. I hadn't really eaten, so I told her to stop so I could get something to put on my stomach.

We pulled in the drive-thru at Zaxby's, and she ordered us something to eat. I killed that shit. Hell, I was eating like I hadn't eaten in days.

"Damn, bitch, slow down."

"Fuck you," I mumbled with a mouth full of chicken.

I mean, that shit was good as hell.

We pulled up to the building in no time. As soon as my foot hit the ground, I felt dizzy again. I stood up and fell right back down.

"You OK, Kyndall?" was the last thing I heard before I blacked out.

****

"Look who's up," I heard a guy with a foreign voice say.

I looked around the room, and Danni was nowhere to be found. I was sure she would come back, so I wasn't worried.

"How long was I out?" I asked the doctor as I grabbed the bottle of water that sat on the table next to the bed.

"Just a few hours, but you are OK, though. Since you are up, you can go home. Let me have the nurse bring in your discharge papers and a prescription for your prenatal vitamins."

I damn near choked on the water when he said that shit. He had the wrong sister. There was no way I was pregnant.

"What the hell do I need them for? I'm not pregnant."

"Mrs. Richardson, when you fainted, we ran a series of blood tests, and they confirmed you are pregnant."

I could have fucking died. There was no way I could survive losing another child. I dropped my head. I felt so fucking stupid. I was mad at Keem for getting another woman pregnant, and here I was, pregnant by our best friend. All I could do was cry. I had been avoiding Shawnee, but there was no way I could make it through this without her.

Danni came back into the room right as the nurse was bringing me my discharge papers.

The whole ride, all I could do was think about how I was going to make it through another pregnancy.

"Kyndall, so what did they say was wrong?" Danni asked, pulling me from my thoughts.

"They said I was dehydrated," I lied.

I was happy I was talking to Danni rather than Shawnee because she would have known I was lying. I wanted to tell someone, but

I knew it couldn't be her because she would call Shawnee, and I couldn't have that. So, I planned to call Mom-Mom Ella as soon as I got home. A part of me wished I could call Cash and tell him. I wanted him so bad. It was so bad that all I did was think about him.

Deep down, I was happy that there was a chance I was going to give him his first child, but then the thought of going through the same thing I had just gone through invaded my mind, and I wasn't sure if I wanted to keep this baby.

Chapter five

Nadia

All I had been doing was crying ever since Cash had spared my life. He had had me held captive in one of his homes with Mrs. Lucille looking after me. She was a very nice lady, and she had been holding me while I cried every night.

Cash might not have killed me, but I knew my days were numbered. When the doctors came in to see me, they confirmed that I was fourteen weeks pregnant, which shocked the hell out of me. This confirmed that my baby was indeed Cash's baby, which caused me to cry even more.

"Come on, baby, you have to stop crying and eat something," Mrs. Lucille said, entering my room.

"I'm not hungry, Mrs. Lucille."

"Listen, girl, Cashmere's evil ass is never going to forgive you at all, so the relationship y'all once had is over. What you need to be trying to do is figure out something to do with your life before this baby gets here."

"For what? All he is going to do is kill me anyway and raise his kid alone."

"Cash may seem like that, but he's not. So, what we gon' do while you are in my care is get you right. Shit, the reason you're in this situation is because of what you did, and the fact of the matter is, there's no turning back. Now, moving forward, you have a little person to live for, so get up and go shower and come down for breakfast. Today is the day you start working on a better you, and I'll work on Cashmere letting you live."

Mrs. Lucille was right, and I swear she was just what I needed at a time like this.

 I got up and made my way to the bathroom so I could shower. Once I made it to the bathroom, I turned the water on to the temperature I liked, then jumped in. After washing and rinsing a couple of times, I now felt refreshed. I got out and dried off. While I was drying off, I noticed my little pudge starting to stick out.

 I walked over to the floor-length mirror that hung on the back of the bathroom door and turned sideways. The sight of my stomach starting to grow made me all emotional. I swear I was a big-ass crybaby since I had been pregnant.

I wrapped the towel around my waist and headed into the room. After grabbing the lotion off the dresser and some underclothes out of the drawer, I sat on the bed and began to lotion my skin. Once I was finished, I slipped my underclothes on, then walked over to the closet to find something to put on.

While I was in the closet, I heard the door open, and I assumed it was Mrs. Lucille.

"I was coming down in a second, Mrs. Lucille."

 When she didn't respond, I turned around and noticed Cash was standing in the doorway. Seeing him angered me so much, I sucked my teeth and turned back around to look in the closet.

"Turn around," he said while staring at my stomach.

We both stood in silence for a second while he gawked at my little pudge.

"Umm, can I put my clothes on now?"

"Go ahead. How far along are you?"

"The doctor came by this morning and told me I was fourteen weeks."

Cash's eyes popped out of his head.

"Damn, ma, you're that far along?"

"Yes, and I know for sure it's your baby. I know you'll never forgive me, and I'm starting to come to grips with that. I also know that you plan to kill me after I give birth. Now, I know you will be the best father you can be, but please at least let he or she know my name. I may not have been good for anything else, but if I'm ever able to experience motherhood, I'ma make sure I'm the best I can be because I never had a good upbringing."

I know what y'all are thinking, and I know I had a chance at motherhood before, but I was young, and I wasn't ready. With this child, I had a second chance at it, and I was going to try my hardest.

Feeling Cash still standing there, watching me, made me uncomfortable.

I looked up at him, and we made eye contact, but he never spoke. We just stared into each other's eyes. His eyes were so sad, and I could tell he hadn't been sleeping. I guess this shit with Kyndall had been taking a toll on him. Yeah, I knew what had gone down because Mrs. Lucille told me.

After finding out about the big old love triangle that was going on, I felt like shit. We all had one big-ass orgy going on and didn't even know it.

Even though I had never given a damn about Kyndall, I felt bad at the moment. Seeing how sad he was, I thought maybe he did need her. Thinking like that made me emotional, and here came the waterworks. I swear crying had become the new norm for me.

Cash didn't say shit. He looked at me, turned around and headed back downstairs.

When he left out, I started wiping my tears away and putting my clothes on. I had to get over Cashmere Whitfield and move on with whatever bit of life I had left. He didn't have to accept my apology, but I felt a little bit better now that he had heard it.

 I decided on a big sweatshirt and tights and threw on my fluffy socks.

Cash made sure Mrs. Lucille had everything I needed here, which was shocking to me. He could have made sure I didn't have a motherfucking thing, but he did. I mean, I had all my toiletries, favorite foods, and comfortable clothes. He wouldn't give me a phone or computer, but Mrs. Lucille said I could use hers, but only to do something that was beneficial. So, I was thinking about starting some online classes. Shit, I didn't have anything but time on my hands.

"You finally made it downstairs. You didn't fuck that boy again, did you?"

"No, Mrs. Lucille, I didn't," I giggled.

"Good, because y'all two need to go your separate ways. The only time y'all need to communicate is when it has to do with that baby."

"I know, Mrs. Lucille. It's going to be a long journey for me, but hearing what you told me earlier, I know I need to get myself together."

This little person was going to change my whole world, either for the good or the bad, and I was praying for the good. I just had to pray that Cash spared my life after I gave birth.

Keem

Today was the day I was going home, and I couldn't wait, even though I hated that I was going to be alone. Chrissy tried to get me to stay at her house, but I wasn't beat for that. I had already set up for a visiting nurse to come out. Right now, I needed help to move around, and I couldn't move fast without getting out of breath. Granted, I knew I needed Chrissy, I just didn't want to be bothered.

There was a knock at the door, and I just sat and waited to see who was going to enter.

A tall, light-skinned man entered the room and spoke.

"Hello, are you Hakeem Richardson?"

"Yes, and you are?"

"I'm Steven Jones, and you've been served."

He handed me a yellow envelope and headed back out the door. I opened the envelope, and my heart dropped. Kyndall had filed for divorce. The crazy part was, no one knew where her ass was, but apparently, the lawyer did.

I laid back on the bed, pissed the fuck off. My life was all fucked up, and it was my own fault.

My room door opened again, and I was shocked at who walked in this time.

"So, what brings you here? Did you come to finish the job?" I asked Cash.

"Nigga, if I wanted you dead, you would be, so don't tempt me, motherfucker," Cash snapped.

"All I wanna know is why, bro? We were tight as hell, so why did you not only find the need to start stealing from me, but fuck my girl and chance her baby being yours?" I looked at him with a raised eyebrow.

"You slept with my wife, so we're even. But as far as me stealing from you, you should know me better than that."

"Nigga, I don't know you at all, so don't tell me I know you."

"Cash, man, I'm not having a good day, so I would like it if you left."

"Keem, I don't give a fuck what you would like. I ain't leaving until I'm good and damn ready."

"Well, since you won't leave, let's talk. How long have you been fucking my wife? Don't lie and tell me it hasn't been long or a couple of times because I ain't buying that shit."

"To be honest with you, we slept together twice, and yeah, I love her. You shouldn't care, though, because you didn't want her."

Hearing him say that had me fucking furious. I didn't even respond, I just laid my head back and looked out the window.

"Well, do me a favor since I know you probably know where she is. Tell her I ain't granting her no fucking divorce, so I don't know why she sent them papers to me."

Cash's eyes lit up as if he had just found out the best news of his life.

"What you mean? Where she at? Did she call you? I swear if you don't tell me where she at, I'ma kill ya stupid ass."

 He ran over to me, pulled a gun out and put it to my head.

This nigga was gone off my wife.

"I ain't telling you shit, so if you gon' kill me, go right ahead, player."

"Yo, man, it took forever to find a parking spot around this bitch," Luke said while walking in.

He looked at Cash and ran straight over to the both of us.

"You don't love her, man. You never did, so why won't you just tell me where she is, so I can talk to her?"

"Cash, give me the gun, man. You're in a fucking hospital. As much as I hate this sucka-ass clown, killing him ain't even worth it. Kyndall will never forgive you if you do this."

The minute Cash heard Kyndall's name, it looked like he had softened up, but not before he hit me in my nose with the gun. Blood splattered everywhere, and I screamed like a bitch.

"You gon' grant her that divorce, or you gon' die, then she won't need one," Cash said while he and Luke walked out of the door.

I wasn't paying his ass any mind. I guess he would have to kill me then because I wasn't granting her shit. What did I look like letting my wife and my best friend live happily ever after? Shit, I knew I had fucked up, but I would rather her be alone if she wasn't going to fix things with me.

I pushed the button for the nurse to come check my nose out; I was sure my shit was broken.

Chapter six

Chrissy

Keem had been really pushing me away, and I wasn't feeling the shit at all. He had been released from the hospital and didn't even want me to help take care of him. It had been nearly a week, and I had been blowing him up.

"What you in here thinking about?" Keys asked.

I had been chilling with him for the past week or so. I knew I was wrong, but the truth of the matter was, I had been lonely with no one to talk to.

"Oh, nothing! I'm hungry as hell."

"Well, get dressed so we can go out to eat."

He didn't have to tell me twice. I jumped up so I could go get ready.

Keys caught me off guard by standing there, staring at me.

"Why are you looking at me like that?"

"Looking at that belly starting to poke out. Have you been to the doctor yet?"

"Not since I first found out. I've been so busy trying to make sure Keem was good that it's really slipped my mind."

"That's my baby, Chrissy, so you need to stop catering to that nigga. If my baby is born with any type of birth defect, I'ma kill you and that nigga."

Keys was so sure this baby was his, while I kept convincing myself that it wasn't his. I knew it really was, but I wasn't ready for that news. This was the real reason I hadn't been to the doctor: I knew the truth, and that shit was going to hurt. If this baby were indeed Keys', Keem and I would never be. I wasn't ready to deal with that since I had done so much to get this man.

Not paying him any mind, I headed to the bathroom to shower. I made sure to lock the bathroom door. See, Keys had been trying to fuck, but I refused. I couldn't lie and say that I didn't want him, but I knew it was going to get his feelings more involved, and I didn't need that.

"OK," was all I could say.

I didn't feel like arguing with him today, so I let him have it. Once I was dressed and ready to go, I grabbed my purse. Just as I was walking out, my phone rang, and I saw that it was Keem. I wanted to answer, but I knew Keys would be walking out the door at any moment.

I hit ignore and blocked his number because I knew he would be calling back. During the whole ride, Keys talked, and I couldn't tell you shit he had said. All I could think about was Keem. I had never been so in love with someone before. I just wanted this meal to be over so I could get to Keem.

We pulled up to Olive Garden in no time. I already knew what I wanted, so I wasted no time when we were seated.

"Damn, baby, you must really be hungry."

"Yes."

I knew he was going to get in his feelings, but I didn't care because I was already in mine. Once we were done eating, I just knew we were going back to the house, but I was fooled. This nigga stopped at his mama's house. When he cut the car off, I just sat there, playing on my phone because there was no way I was going in that house with him. His mama hated me, and I had no idea why.

"Come on," he said, opening the door so I could get out.

I looked at his ass like he had three heads.

"I'm not going in there. You know yo' mama don't fuck with me," I said with an attitude.

I hope he got the point and stopped trying because I wasn't going in there.

"Look, baby, she just hasn't gotten to know you yet."

"I'm not going, so you can go and talk to her, and I will wait," I told him in the calmest tone.

He just sighed and closed the door.

As soon as he was in the house, I called Keem.

"Why the fuck haven't you been answering the fucking phone?" he snarled as soon as he answered.

I knew he was going to be pissed.

"I'm sorry, baby, I was busy," I lied.

"You need to get to my house in the next hour," was all he said before hanging up.

I ordered an Uber and prayed Keys didn't come out the house before I could leave. Luckily, my Uber only took five minutes to get to me.

As soon as I saw the car, I hurried and walked to the end of the driveway. I knew Keys was going to be mad, but all I had to do was fuck him, and he would forget all about me leaving.

The ride to Keem's house took all of forty-five minutes, which meant I had gotten there in time. When I walked into the house, it was a mess. I was sure he hadn't cleaned up since he had been home.

I walked through the house to the room that he and Kyndall shared. He was laid out on the bed, and the room smelled like a locker room. I went to the bathroom and cut the shower on so he could bathe.

"Keem, baby, come on and get up so you can shower," I urged.

It took him a while, but he finally got up and dragged to the bathroom. I got him a towel out the linen closet and closed the door, so he could shower.

I walked back into the room and stood in the middle of the room to try to figure out where to start cleaning. I decided to change the sheets on the bed, then proceeded to pick up all the shit that was all over the floor.

I knew I was going to be tired, but I needed him to know I had his back.

Once I was done in the room, and he was done showering, I headed to the living room to do the same. I also wanted to cook him something to eat. I knew that once I took care of him, he would love me the way he used to love Kyndall.

Shawnee

"Nee-Nee, can we eat pizza today?" Joi asked as she came into the room.

I had been in bed all day, feeling sick as hell.

"Yes, baby, go and get the coupons off the fridge so I can order the pizza."

"Yes, ma'am."

Joi was such a happy little girl. I swear she gave me life. Some days, I wondered how Meia functioned without her. If I ever had kids, I would make sure I loved them so much, they would never question it.

I sat up in bed and called Luke so I could see what time he was coming home. It was getting late, and he hadn't called me like he normally did.

"Hey, baby. You feeling better?" he asked as soon as he answered.

"Not really. How long before you come home? Me and Joi are ordering pizza, and I was hoping you could bring me a pineapple Fanta and bring Joi a Jungle Juice."

"OK, baby, I'm on my way now," he assured me.

See, that was one of the things I loved about my baby: he made sure the world stopped for Joi and me.

We ended the call, and I got up and headed to check on Joi because it had been a while since she went downstairs.

I walked into the living room and didn't see her.

"Joi, baby, where are you?" I yelled through the house.

When I walked into the kitchen, she was on the floor, crying, and the patio door was opened. I ran straight to her.

"Baby, what's wrong?" I asked.

"I don't want my mommy to be my mommy anymore. She took my phone and my necklace Daddy gave me. Daddy's going to whoop me because he said not to let anyone take it off me!" she cried.

I closed the patio door, then called Luke. He didn't answer, so I called Cash.

"What's good, sis?" he answered.

"I have been calling Luke. He didn't answer. Can you come to the house?"

There was nothing else that needed to be said. He ended the call.

I picked Joi up and carried her to the living room. The entire time we sat there, I asked myself what the fuck Meia was thinking. She knew Luke was going to kill her. That man didn't play about Joi. He would probably go to war with God about her. Meia was really pushing it. Who does shit like this? The necklace was worth almost ten thousand dollars, so I knew he was going to flip. He told me the other day that he thought she was on drugs, but I was sure he would know for sure now.

"Baby, what the fuck happened?" Luke asked as he and Cash walked into the door at the same time.

I just looked down at Joi. She was playing with my phone, so she wasn't paying attention when he first walked in.

As soon as she heard his voice, she jumped up and ran straight to him and Cash. She was holding on to each of their legs. Cash picked her up. As soon as he asked what was wrong, she started crying.

"Mommy came, and she took my necklace and my phone."

Luke's face turned red as hell, and so did Cash's.

Cash took her upstairs, so I knew that meant Luke was about to go in on me.

"How the fuck did that happen?" he asked me as soon as they made it up the stairs.

"I told her to go and get the coupons for the pizza. When she didn't come right back, I came to look for her. She was in the kitchen by the door, crying. She then told me the same thing that she just told y'all. My thing is, how did Meia know where we lived? You told me she didn't know about this house!" I damn near yelled.

I was pissed. When I agreed to move in with him, he assured me that she didn't know where he lived. That bitch could have taken Joi and killed me.

"I don't fucking know, Shawn. I told you she hadn't ever been to this house!" he yelled back.

I didn't have shit else to say.

I went upstairs and got Joi and pushed past Cash. I knew it wasn't his fault, but I didn't care.

I packed Joi a bag, then got dressed. There was no way we were staying here.

After I was dressed, I went to the room and got Joi. We headed to the front door.

"Where the fuck you think y'all going?" Luke asked.

I stopped and looked at him like he was crazy.

"To my house until you find us a new one. She could have taken my baby and did something to me. There is no way we are staying here. Now, you may not feel like you have to leave, but we are."

"So, you gon' just take my baby?" he smiled.

My heart fluttered. There was something about that man's smile that made me fall deeper in love with him every time he displayed it.

I walked out the door. He knew where to find us. As soon as we got in the car, I gave Joi my phone, and we headed to AT&T so I could get my baby a new phone.

"Come on, baby, so we can get you a new phone," I said, helping her out the car.

She looked so happy, and that was all I wanted.

"Can I call you Mommy, Nee-Nee, because I want you to be my mommy?" she asked as we walked into the store, hand in hand.

"We will have to talk to Daddy about it, but if he's OK with it, then I am as well. Now, what kind of phone do you want?"

"I want one like yours."

I smiled and told the clerk to give me an iPhone 8 Plus, and he looked at me like I was crazy. I just shrugged and sat down. It took them nearly an hour to get the phone set up and for Joi to find a case like mine. I had a purple OtterBox, and she chose a pink one.

After that, we headed to get something to eat. I knew she was going to want The Cheesecake Factory, so I headed in that direction.

As we were getting ready to pull up, Luke called and asked where we were. I told him we were going to eat, so he already knew what restaurant we were headed to. As soon as we pulled into the parking space, he was walking up to the car to help us get out.

Chapter seven

Luke

I knew Shawnee was mad, but she didn't have to go as far as telling me that I needed to buy a whole new fucking house. I think the one we lived in was just fine.

"Well, looks like you need to be calling Ben so you can sell this little bitty shack," Cash joked.

He was always going in on my damn house. He said I made too much money to live in a house this small and in this neighborhood. I'd had this house for years. It was the first thing I bought when I started getting money.

"Nigga, fuck you. I don't need all that house like you got. Who the fuck lives alone, but has six fucking bedrooms? That shit is creepy as hell," I laughed.

I hated sleeping at that nigga's house. Don't get me wrong, I was not a scary nigga at all, but I didn't like creepy shit. My house was small enough to know what the fuck was going on at all times.

"Well, yo' ass getting one now, 'cause you know she gon' buy the biggest one she can find."

He was laughing hard as hell, and I wanted to shoot his ass.

"Fuck you."

We had just left Meia's house, looking for her coke head ass. I couldn't wait to lay my eyes on her. She knew better than to play with my baby. Then, to top that off, she broke into my house. There was no telling what she had taken. Shawnee was worried about Joi, so she probably didn't even look.

When I left her house, I went to her mom's house, but no one came to the door, so I headed back home so Cash could get in his own car. I knew I was going to catch up with her sooner or later, I just hoped she enjoyed her last few days living.

We talked for a little longer, then I called Shawnee. I wanted to see what she and Joi were doing. She told me they were getting something to eat, so I knew just where they were. Joi only ate at one place, so I got in my car and headed there. It took me no time because I was right down the street from the house.

When I pulled up, I saw Shawnee's Porsche pulling into a parking space. I jumped out my car so I could help her get Joi out the car. I couldn't help but smile. I had the perfect family.

"Hey, Daddy. Can I call Nee-Nee Mommy because I need her to be my mommy?"

I had to do a double take. I looked at Shawnee, and she just shrugged her shoulders. I really didn't know how to answer her because I didn't know how Shawnee felt. I figured she had already said something to Shawnee.

I took a deep breath. "Yes, baby, you can call her whatever you want," I assured her.

When I said that, Joi jumped up and down. All we could do was laugh.

When we walked into the restaurant, Joi went to the hostess's desk.

"We need a table for me, Mommy and Daddy," she told the girl.

I just shook my head because my baby wanted to be a big girl so bad.

The lady sat us at our booth and took our drink orders. Joi always wanted Sprite, but this time, she said she wanted water because that was what Shawnee was getting. This was life. No matter what I did in the streets, none of that mattered when I was around these two. I just wished I had met Shawnee sooner so she could have been my baby mother. What she didn't know was that I was going to make her way more than my baby mama. She was going to be my wife.

"Baby, I was looking at this house when I was getting Joi's new phone," she said, handing me her phone.

My eyes damn near popped out my head.

"Shawn, this damn house is 2.5 million dollars. Why do you need a house that cost that damn much? Hell, that's too many damn rooms. It's me, you and Joi. We don't need that much space. We can find a nice three-bedroom house," I told her.

She was pouting and shit.

Joi took the phone from my hand. She scanned the pictures of the house, then gave it back to me.

"Well, Daddy, I think we can get that house and you and Mommy can have me a sister to play with, and you can get me a big pool like Uncle Cash, and I can have two rooms, and my sister can have one room, and Tee-Tee Kyn can come and live with us."

I just shook my head because they were really double-teaming me.

"We will see."

"OK, good, because I talked to the realtor that helped me find my house. We were going to look at it when we leave here."

"So, you just knew I was going to say yes?"

"Yep."

She kissed me, and my dick sprang up. I had to adjust myself because Joi was here. If it had been just Shawnee and me, we would have been in the bathroom fucking.

"Can I take your order?" the waiter asked.

We gave her our orders and looked at a few more houses while we waited.

I was excited about getting a house with Shawnee, but she wouldn't know that. I had to wait until Kyndall came back so I could ask Shawnee to be my wife. The only reason I said that was because it just wouldn't be right if her cousin weren't here.

After we were done eating, they got in the car with me, and I called Cash so he could pick Shawnee's car up. The car was quiet on the way to the house because Joi was asleep.

"Where did that question come from?" I asked, pulling Shawnee's attention from her phone.

"What question?" she asked, locking her phone and putting it in the cup holder.

I loved the fact that she wasn't attached to her phone like most females.

"That Joi asked."

"Oh. I don't know. She asked me the same thing, and I told her we would have to talk to you about it."

"I was just asking, baby. I'm rocking with whatever you're rocking with. I just hope this house looks like what it does on the internet. That shit far as hell," I complained.

It really wasn't that far, I just didn't want to spend that much on a house. The truth was, the house wasn't far from the warehouse, so that would be a plus.

"Look, Daddy!" Joi yelled, scaring the hell out of me.

Shawnee saw me jump, so I knew she was going to tease me about that shit for the next week. I was driving, so I didn't really pay attention to the houses that we were passing. All of them were huge and gated.

We pulled up to the address Shawn had put in the GPS, and I was at a loss for words. The picture didn't do this house any justice.

"Come on, Daddy," Joi said, climbing in the front seat like she always did.

She didn't like getting out the back door. She said that was for little kids and that she was a big girl.

"Hey, Shawnee. Girl, you're glowing! Let me find out you got a bun in the oven," the realtor said as she greeted us.

"Girl, no. This is my boyfriend, Luke, and our daughter, Joi."

"Hey, how you guys doing?"

"Good, now can I go see my new room because Daddy's buying Mommy and me this house and we get a pool, too. Right, Daddy?"

I just nodded and followed them into the house. I was amazed at how nice the house was. I knew I was going to have to cut a check for this today. If not, I wasn't going to get any pussy later, and I couldn't have that.

I watched in amazement at how happy they were, and that was what mattered to me.

"We will take it," Shawnee said when we finished.

"Yep, we will take it," Joi mocked Shawnee.

I just laughed and told her to submit an offer.

This was life.

Nadia

Even though I was still held captive in Cash's house, I was in great spirits. My online classes started, I was eating, and the baby was growing well. I still hadn't seen Cash since the day he had left, but I wasn't really worried about him.

"What you in here doing, mama?" Mrs. Lucille asked.

"Nothing, just laying here thinking about how my life is about to change for the better as long as I'm still living."

"Would you stop saying that? You'll be fine. Cash is not going to harm you."

"I wish I could believe you, Mrs. Lucille, but the Cash I know doesn't take no shit."

The whole time she had been here, she had been trying to assure me that Cash wasn't going to kill me. I didn't believe that at all.

"What y'all in here doing?" Cash asked, making us both jump.

"Boy, don't be just walking in here like that, scaring the hell out of me," Mrs. Lucille fussed.

I could still see the sadness in his eyes, but he looked better than the last time I had seen him. His dreads were twisted nicely, and he had a fresh lineup.

Nadia, stop gawking over this nigga, I said to myself before turning my head.

"My fault, Mrs. Lucille. Can I talk to Nadia alone, please?"

She gave him the side-eye and hesitated to get up.

Cash laughed at her and shook his head.

"As long as you're just talking and she's keeping her legs closed. You know I can't leave you two alone."

"I'm good, Mrs. Lucille. I know how to keep my legs closed."

She got up and walked out of the room.

"So, now you figured out how to keep them legs closed?"

"Look, Cashmere, I'm finally trying to get my head on straight, so arguing with you is out of the question. I know what I did was wrong, and we will never get back together. My days are coming to an end, and I wish you would just let me live my little bit of life free. What's your reason for keeping me locked up? You don't fucking want me."

"You're here because you don't know how to fucking act. If that is my baby, there's no way I'ma let you outside so you can be out here busting it wide open for just anybody with my seed growing in you. My feelings were all fucked up because of how you did me, Nadia. Not to mention, knowing the baby we were happy about might not be mine. How am I supposed to feel now?"

"Nigga, don't come at me like that when you know good and damn well your little feelings are hurt because Kyndall's ass is nowhere around. So, save that bullshit, Cashmere. Yeah, I fucked up, and I'm not gon' keep apologizing for what I did. This baby is yours, and he or she will be here soon."

The minute I said that, I felt a kick from the baby and grabbed my stomach.

Cash ran over to me with a worried expression on his face.

"Are you OK?"

"Yes, the baby just kicked. Let me see your hand."

He gave me his hand, and I put it on the side where the baby was moving. Once the baby kicked again, his face lit up, and a smile crept across his face.

"Nadia, I fucked up, and I'm sorry. For years, you kept saying that me and Kyndall loved each other and I kept telling you we didn't. To be honest with you, I really didn't know how I felt, and for that, I dragged you along. We both fucked up, but we really need to get our shit together for this baby."

"I totally agree, Cash, but us being together is not happening. I know now your heart is with Kyndall, so co-parenting is fine with me. If we continued dealing with each other, all we would do is continue to hurt one another."

"I'm cool with that, but I want you to stay with me until you have the baby."

"No, I'm good with staying here. I just need my car back so I can get around."

"OK, I'll have it towed here later on."

"All right, cool, so does that mean you not gon' kill me?"

He chuckled and started shaking his head.

"I was never going to kill you, ma, I just didn't want you out in these streets doing me dirty."

"Ya crazy ass was about to kill me until Luke stopped you."

"I wasn't in my right state of mind then. I'm good now. I'm just tryna maintain and get my shit together before this baby gets here. Oh, yeah, I wanna take you to see my mama."

"Cashmere, you know ya mama don't like me."

"I know, but she knows you're having her first grand, and she wants to talk to you."

"Oh, so you believe this is your baby now?"

"Yeah, I believe you, and besides, you know how crazy I am. If you lie, you know I'll kill you with no remorse."

"All right. Well, let me know when we going to see your mom."

"Now. Get dressed. I'll wait for you downstairs."

Chapter Eight

Cash

Having a long talk with my mom today and then feeling my baby move in Nadia's stomach put me in a better mood today, but I had still been in my feelings about not knowing where Kyndall's stubborn ass was. She needed to do better. It was as if every time shit was going rough, she ran away from her problems. Yeah, shit got real, and people got hurt, but she had family here and people who loved and missed her.

"How you been doing, baby?" Mrs. Lucille asked me, taking me out of my thoughts.

"I'm OK, just trying to get my shit together."

"Boy, you better watch your mouth while talking to me."

"I'm sorry, Mrs. Lucille. I didn't mean for that to come out that way."

"I'ma tell you this. If it's meant to be with that girl Kyndall, then she'll make her way back to you. Until then, you need to get on with your life. This is not the Cashmere I know. He would not let anything get him down like this."

I didn't say anything, I just listened to what she said. Luke had been drilling the same exact thing in my head. Hearing them say that just made me mad because Kyndall was all I had wanted lately. Shit, the saying the truth hurt was true for me these days.

"Are you ready to go?" Nadia asked, taking me out of my thoughts.

I looked up at her and stared for a minute. My baby had her so beautiful; she wore a PINK sweatshirt, a pair of tights, and some UGGS. Mrs. Lucille had called me a week ago and told me Nadia needed some more clothes because her belly was getting bigger. Seeing her today confirmed that she was indeed getting big. That shit happened fast as hell. It was as if one minute she found out she was pregnant, then the next, she got big. The doctor did say she was fourteen weeks when she found out, so that meant she had been pregnant and didn't know.

See, Nadia didn't know the doctor reported to me after every visit, and that was how I knew the baby was mine.

Mrs. Lucille cleared her throat, and I looked up at her.

"My fault, ma, come on, let's go."

"Where y'all headed to?"

"We're gonna go see my mom."

"OK, tell Della I said hello, and I'll give her a call later."

Nadia walked over to Mrs. Lucille and gave her a hug and kiss, then headed out the door. I knew she was anxious to get out since it had been a while. I noticed she and Lucille had been getting close, and that was a good thing to me because Nadia didn't have a loving mother and father. They both were on bullshit.

 Once we made it out to the car, I opened the door for her and made sure she was in safely, then I headed around to the driver's side. I jumped in and peeled off.

A half hour later...

We were now pulling up to my parents' house. My dad was back home for a little bit, so I wanted to do dinner with them. They knew about everything that had happened, and they were very disappointed in me for shooting Keem and Kyn. They said I was mad, but I should have controlled my anger.

"Hey, son, how are you feeling?" my pops asked as soon as I walked into the house.

"I'm good, Pops, just trying to keep my head above water."

"You're a Whitfield, baby! You are as strong as an ox. This all will pass soon. Hey, pretty lady, how are you and my grandbaby doing?" he asked Nadia.

"I'm fine, just a little tired and always hungry. The baby is growing well. Today, Cash and I felt the baby move for the first time, and I'm almost five months. We should find out what we are having at the next appointment."

"You're so far along. Why did you wait so long to tell my son you were pregnant?" my mom fussed as she walked into the living room.

"Della, don't start your shit. Leave that girl alone. Cash told us it's his baby and that's all that matters. When and why he's just now finding out is none of our business."

She rolled her eyes and went back into the kitchen. My mom was not happy about this at all. She was Team Kyndall and was praying she returned soon, but the fact of the matter was, if Kyndall came back or not, Nadia and I still had a baby on the way.

"Come on, Ma, you can sit down right here."

I knew my mom was just in her feelings, but we weren't leaving. My mom didn't have to ever like her, but she needed to keep it cordial when they were around each other.

After Nadia sat down, I left her in the living room with my pops while I went to have a couple of words with my mom.

"Hey, Mom, what's up?"

"Don't come in here giving me that look, Cashmere. You already know how I feel about all of this."

"I know, Mama, and I know you don't want anything to do with her, but we are about to have a baby. You have to get along for my seed, Mom."

"I'll give it a chance, Cash, for the sake of my grandbaby. I'ma tell you this, though; she better be the best mommy she can be because I ain't got no problem with taking and raising my grandbaby."

My mom was dead ass serious, so I hoped Nadia was ready. After talking to my mom a little more, I headed back to the living room with my pops and Nadia.

"What y'all in here talking about?"

"Ms. Nadia was telling me how she was doing online classes right now."

What my pops said was all new to me.

"Really, ma? That's what's up!"

After we sat and talked a little more, my mother called us into the dining room for dinner. We all sat at the table, and she brought us a plate over. My pops said grace, and we all dug in.

"So, Nadia, what are your plans after the baby?"

"Well, I just started online classes a couple of weeks ago, so I plan on continuing with that. Then, when the baby gets older, I plan on having my business degree right along with a couple of other degrees. After that, hopefully, I'll be able to open up a couple of beauty supply stores in the city. Most of the beauty supply stores are owned by Chinese. We need some more black-owned businesses in Camden."

Nadia was shocking the hell out of me, and I knew Mrs. Lucille had gotten to her.

"That's good. Well, when the baby is born, me and Carson will be around to help Cash and you as much as we can. As long as you're doing right for yourself and my grandbaby, I'll have your back."

Hearing my mom say that made me smile. I knew it took a lot out of her to say that, but I knew she would do anything for me. We all ate and talked some more. Before I knew it, it was late as hell, so Nadia and I ended up staying at my parents' house and sleeping in the spare bedroom.

Meia

"Bitch, wake ya simple ass up!" Tory fussed while he slapped me in my face.

"What, man? Why you hitting me like that?"

"Your simple ass smoked up all my shit. Now you gon' have to work it off. This little necklace you got from your baby daddy is not enough. I have another plan up my sleeve."

It was too early in the morning for this guy's shit. Yeah, I knew I had fucked up, but shit, my days were numbered. Either he was going to kill me, or Luke was.

My name is Meia Thomas, and I am twenty-eight years old. I was born and raised in Philadelphia but moved to Camden when I met Luke. He and I used to be madly in love until this Shawnee chick came along.

After Luke kicked me to the curb, I started hanging out at these traps in the city. That was how I had met Tory and his boy, Keys. One night, they had a party, and my ass smoked one of Tory's blunts that was laced with coke. Now, here I was, a fucking coke head.

My daughter didn't even want to see me anymore. I had been following Shawnee around for a couple of weeks, and that was how I knew where they'd been staying. Watching her interact with my baby and her call her mom infuriated me, but there was nothing I could do about it. Shit, she was better off with people who could love her and take care of her, unlike my coke head ass.

"Bitch, do you hear me talking to you?"

"Tory, I hear you. Please just let me get a little more sleep, then we can discuss what else we can do to get your money."
"If ya simple ass had been a good baby mama, you could have been getting a good penny for child support, but you had to be one of those trifling-ass mothers."

"Nigga, FUCK YOU! Figure that shit out yourself!" I snapped.

He jumped on me so fast. He slapped my face, then grabbed my neck.

"You gon' stop talking to me like I'm some bitch-ass nigga like ya baby daddy."

I looked at him and laughed so hard.

"Nigga, please, ain't a bitch-ass bone in my baby daddy's body. What's the beef you got with Luke? You've been talking slick about him since I first met you."

"I ain't got no beef with his punk ass."

"Yeah, OK. It's some hate there somewhere."

Tory was saying some off the wall shit about Luke, but he wouldn't tell me what the beef was. Something was up with him, and I wondered what it was. Him slapping me and grabbing me by my neck had me wanting to fuck him.

I jumped up and headed to the bathroom to take care of my hygiene and brush my teeth. Twenty minutes went by, and I was now walking back into the room with a towel wrapped around my body.

Tory was still sitting on the side of the bed, into his phone, not paying me any mind. I walked over to him and let the towel drop to my feet and straddled him. He looked at me and smiled while palming my ass cheek with his free hand.

"What you doing, girl?"

"What does it look like I'm doing? I'm trying to get you to fuck me," I said while nibbling on his ear and kissing his neck.

Tory and I engaged in a passionate kiss while he rubbed both of my breasts. While he was showing my breasts all the attention, I unbuttoned his pants, unleashing the beast.

Once his dick was out and poking at my opening, I slid right down on it with no hesitation. The feeling of him inside of me felt so amazing. I bounced on top of him in a fast motion, trying to get this nut off. Tory kept grabbing my waist to slow me down, but I didn't want to slow down.

"Come on, ma, slow ya little ass down. I ain't ready to cum yet!" he barked, but I wasn't paying his ass any mind.

"Shut up and fuck me back!" I sassed.

Tory did as I said, and now we were matching each other's stroke.

"Yessssss, baby, just like that," I cooed in his ear.

Sex with Tory was amazing. He just couldn't keep his hands to himself. Little did he know, my ass was batshit crazy, and I would just laugh at his ass. I felt my nut coming, so I started tightening my pussy muscles on Tory. I wanted us to bust this nut together.

"Fuck! Meia, I'm about to cum, baby."

"I'm cumming, too, Tory."

After we both came long and hard, we just sat there for a minute, trying to catch our breath.

"So, since I gave you some of this good-ass dick, are you ready to hear my plan now?"

"What is it, Tory?"

"You fucked up a lot of my money, and I want my shit back. Granted, we deal with each other the long way. How about we come up with a plan where we both can get a come up?"

I was all ears. I wasn't getting any money from Luke because he always had Joi, so my bank account was empty. Tory was mad at me for smoking up a large quantity of his shit, so he wasn't giving me anything. Hell, he could get the money I owed him, plus, I could get my own money.

"All right, what's the plan?"

"I was thinking we could kidnap baby girl and set a ransom."

After thinking for a couple of minutes, I thought, what the hell, she was my baby anyway, so it was not kidnapping. They would just have to give me some money if they wanted to see her again.

"If we gon' do this, we have to think everything out, detail by detail. This is not something we can just jump into. It really has to be a drawn-out plan," I assured Tory. After we discussed the plan a little, we ended up fucking again, and this time was better than the first time.

We both fell asleep and slept the whole day away.

Chapter nine

Kyndall
(four months later)

I missed my family like crazy. I was playing the role like nothing mattered, when the truth was, all I wanted was to be around Shawnee and Cash, especially since I had found out I was pregnant a few weeks ago. I hadn't even told Danni because I knew she had been talking to Shawnee.

Today, I was going to see a specialist. I had been doing research, and Memphis had some of the best OBGYNs. The lady I was going to see was going to help me carry my baby full term. We had been talking over the phone, but today, she had me coming in so that she could run a few tests on me.

"Hey, boo, where you headed?" Danni asked as she took a seat on my bed.

"To the doctor. I haven't really had a checkup since I lost Nevaeh," I lied.

She gave me a weird look, but I just laughed it off.

Once she left the room, I gave myself a look over and headed out. I wasn't really trying to keep it from anyone, I just didn't want to get too excited because there was a chance I might not make it full term. Everything in me wanted to get an abortion, but I couldn't do it.

When I made it to the appointment, I turned right back around.

I got in the car, and my phone rang. The number said unknown, so I hit ignore. No one knew this number, so I wasn't taking any chances. Cash's reach was long, and I didn't want it to be him. I knew that if I heard his voice, I would be on the first thing smoking back to Camden.

I made it to the doctor's office in no time. I sat in the car for a while and prayed things worked out. I wanted to be a mother so bad. That was all I had ever wanted. I remember when I was younger, I used to tell Cash and Keem I wanted five kids. Cash would laugh and tell me that I liked to shop too much to have that many kids.

"Damn, I miss him," I mumbled out loud as I got out the car.

I was nervous as hell. I mean, my palms were sweating and all. When I walked into the building and saw all the pregnant women, I wanted to cry. I was jealous. I wanted to be just like them.

I signed in, and they called me in no time. When I made it to the back, the tears started to fall.

"Hello, Mrs. Richardson. I am Dr. King, and honey, you don't have to cry. I've read your chart, and I'm here to assure you that you're in the right place. Exactly how many weeks are you?"

"Dr. King, to be honest with you, I have no idea. I haven't been to the doctor because I wasn't sure if I could go through losing another baby."

"I see. Well, today, we can do an ultrasound to see exactly how far along you are. Lay back on the table and pull your shirt above your belly. The gel I have to put on your stomach is going to be cold. OK, Mrs. Richardson, the baby's heartbeat seems to be very strong, and from the baby's measurements, it looks like you're exactly eighteen weeks. Now, usually, the procedure is more effective early in your pregnancy, but it can still be done now. It's a surgery called cerclage, which is when they sew your cervix closed. You will need to be on complete bed rest, then you will take the progesterone shot every week until you're thirty-six weeks. At thirty-six weeks, we will remove the stitches from the cerclage. Now, this is something that will need to be done right away, and I'll be doing it. Your appointment is going to be first thing tomorrow morning at eight."

"OK, Doc, thanks so much. I'll see you then."

"Remember, Mrs. Richardson, no crying and stressing. You have a beautiful bundle of joy to get prepared for."

I wished I could be happy, but I was just too scared about all of this.

I walked out the door when Danni called and told me to meet her at this new spot downtown. I headed straight there because I was beyond hungry.

When I pulled up to the building, Danni was standing at the door, waiting for me. My girl was so beautiful. I had no idea why she didn't have a man. Hell, I was starting to think she was batting for the other side.

"Hey, boo. How was your appointment?"

"It was OK. I'll tell you about it when we get seated."

I knew she was going to kill me because I had been hiding my pregnancy from her.

I sat down but didn't take my jacket off, even though it was warm in the building and outside. When she left my room earlier, I had on my robe because I knew she was coming. Anytime I was around her, I had on an oversized pullover. That was all my ass had been wearing.

"So, what's up?" she asked.

"I have to tell you something, and you can't tell anyone, especially not Shawnee."

She gave me a look I couldn't read, and that made me not want to tell her, but I knew I needed to.

I stood up and took my coat off, and her mouth instantly dropped.

"Bitch, I knew something was up when you stopped drinking. OMG, I'm so happy for you. Why don't you look happy?"

"I'm just scared. I just want my baby to be OK. I don't think I can take losing another baby," I explained.

I knew she wouldn't understand me, but that was fine.

"You'll be fine, Kyn. I told you we have the best doctors out here. What did they tell you at your appointment?"

"Well, she explained a procedure I have to get in the morning. Will you be able to come with me?"

"You know damn well I'm rolling with you until the wheels fall off. Whenever you need me, I'ma be there for our little peanut. Are you sure there are not twins in there because ya ass looks hella big?"

"Bitch, ain't no fucking twins in here," I fussed. Danni and I enjoyed the rest of our afternoon. I loved Danni, but I missed Shawnee so much.

Shawnee

"Baby, you need to shower before everyone gets here!" I yelled across the house to Luke.

He had been on the grill all day so that the food would be ready when the guests got here. It was our first gathering at our new house. We thought about having a housewarming, but since Joi's birthday was so close, we decided to just wait. I had been getting this party together for the past month. My house looked like a unicorn had thrown up. My baby wanted everything to be unicorns. She even wanted people to wear unicorn colors.

I felt like shit, but it was Joi's day, so I had to get my shit in line. Luke had been telling me to go to the doctor, but there was no need for that. I knew what was wrong, but I wasn't ready to face the facts. After I made sure Luke was in the shower, I headed to Joi's room so I could get her dressed. The party was set to start in thirty minutes.

Once she was dressed, and her hair was combed, I sent her downstairs with Luke's mom. I walked into our room and Luke was walking out the bathroom, ass naked. A big-ass smile graced my face. I walked over to him and grabbed his dick, and it sprang straight up.

"What you think you doing?" he smirked.

"Getting some of this good dick."

"You talking about this dick?" he asked, pulling me closer to him.

My pussy was dripping wet. It was so wet, I could feel it through the tights I had on.

"Ummmm."

He was rubbing my clit through my tights, and it was driving me crazy.

"Stop playing and fuck me, Luke," I demanded.

He smirked and pulled my tights down. I knew this was going to have to be quick because Joi would be looking for us soon. She was the queen of cockblocking.

When he slid in me, I swear it felt like the first time. Just as we were getting ready to nut, there was a knock at the door and we both burst out laughing.

"Mommy, Daddy, hurry up!" Joi yelled through the door.

"OK, baby, here we come!" Luke yelled back.

 The funny thing was, he didn't miss a stroke. Once we were done, he got dressed, and I got in the shower. The hot water felt so good beating against my body.

I got dressed and then headed downstairs so I could make sure everything was going good. When I made it to the end of the stairs, my baby ran straight to me.

"Mommy, look at all the gifts I got," she cooed.

"I see, baby."

Just as I said that, I looked up and Cash and Nadia were walking through the door. If looks could kill, his ass would be dead. As soon as he noticed I was looking at him, he dropped his head. I couldn't believe he was back fucking with her duck head ass. That bitch had betrayed him, and he was stupid enough to bring her to my house.

When Joi ran to Cash, that nasty bitch thought she was going to hug my baby, but I put an end to that fast.

"Joi, gon' outside and play, baby."

Cash looked at me like I was crazy, but he knew me better than anyone, so he knew that shit was a no go.

I made sure Joi was outside, then I pulled out my petty side.

"Well, let me go hide my nigga before your hoe tries to fuck him."

Her mouth dropped.

See, she hadn't seen that side of me because I normally didn't talk to her hoe ass. I knew Cash was going to tell Luke, but I didn't care. He better be glad he was Joi's god daddy, or his ass wouldn't be here. He knew I didn't fuck with snake hoes, and Nadia was the leader.

I headed to the kitchen, and they followed. Cash's mom and Luke's mom were in the kitchen, and I knew Luke's mom was going to be just as petty as me.

"Well, that's my cue to go get my man and keep him close. I will see y'all outside," Luke's mom said, causing me and Cash's mom to laugh.

I wanted her to feel uncomfortable. Hell, I prayed she would just leave. She was walking around, rubbing her belly like she was making someone jealous. We all knew that if Kyndall walked through that door right now, he would kick her ass to the curb. One thing we all knew was that his heart belonged to Kyndall.

I missed my boo so much. She had been gone nearly five months, and I was ready for her to come back. I had given her more than enough time to get her mind together. I just wanted her to come back home. I knew something was going on with her because Danni had been acting distant. That meant she was hiding something from me. It was OK because I was going to go and find out myself.

Just as I was getting ready to go in the house and refill the punch, Luke grabbed me.

"Damn, baby, that ass getting fatter."

That was all his nasty ass thought about. I just laughed and headed into the house.

"Cash, why the hell are you on my phone?" I asked as soon as I walked in the door.

"Nothing," he lied.

I knew what he was doing.

"I haven't talked to her, Cash," I told him, rolling my eyes.

I knew he was looking to see if I had been talking to Kyndall, and that was why I had deleted my calls to Danni because that smart motherfucker would have put two and two together.

"And why are you worried about her? You got yo' thot hoe here. You brought that bitch in here like that shit was cool. What if Kyndall was here? Don't bring that hoe to my house again," I fussed.

He knew I wasn't going to bite my tongue.

Cash

I knew Shanwee was going to trip about me bringing Nadia, but I didn't know she was going to be so damn shady. Then, Luke's mom didn't make it any better. I couldn't lie, though. I wanted to laugh so damn bad. I didn't really want to bring Nadia, but things had been going well with us, so I didn't want to argue. I couldn't lie, a nigga was enjoying the new her. She was in school, and that shit shocked me. I was just happy she had decided to change because truthfully, I planned to kill her ass.

"Shawnee, you and I both know that's a lie. You and Mom-Mom Ella both are on good bullshit. Y'all know she's been calling y'all. I just want to know if she's OK," I said.

Just as Shawnee was getting ready to reply, Nadia walked in. I could tell she had heard our conversation. I also knew she was going to be in her feelings.

"I'm ready to go," Nadia said.

I dropped my head. I really didn't mean for her to hear me talking about Kyndall.

"There's the door. I'm sure you have the Uber App. No one is stopping you from traveling, but this is his goddaughter's party so he will be here till it ends. Hell, I don't want yo' ass in my house anyway, so go on and bounce, hoe."

I just shook my head because Shawnee had no filter. The funny thing was, she hadn't stopped making the punch. Hell, she didn't even look at the damn girl.

"I'ma run her to the house, and I will be right back," I said, walking off before Shawnee said something else.

"So, you really let her talk to me like that?"

I knew this was coming.

"Look, baby, that's her house. How the hell am I going to tell her how to talk in her house? I told you before we left the house that you were going to have to put on your tough skin. You fucked her cousin's husband, so you had to know she wasn't going to be all buddy-buddy with you."

I was happy I didn't live that far because I knew Joi would be looking for me. I hit the dash, getting her ass home so I could get back. I didn't want to miss her opening the gift I had gotten her. Luke and I had a bet going to see whose gift she would like the best.

Twenty minutes passed, and we pulled up to the house. She got out and slammed the door. I didn't care, though. She would be OK.

I made it back in record time. They were getting ready to open the gifts.

"Uncle Cash, where have you been? You missed my cake," Joi said when I walked in the house.

"Sorry, baby, I had to drop my friend off," I said, picking her up.

We walked to the back where everyone was.

After we opened gifts, I helped clean up, then I headed home so I could get this argument over between Nadia and me.

I walked in the house, and all the lights were out, which wasn't normal. Nadia hated to be in the dark. Hell, most days, she slept with the TV on so the room wouldn't be dark.

When I made it to our bedroom, she was lying across the bed, ass naked. With the way she was lying, I was able to see her fat ass and her huge belly. I was ready for my little man to get here. We had found out we were having a boy a few months ago, and I was so happy because I had always wanted all boys. For some reason, Kyndall came to my head. I knew she would have been such a great mother.

I took one more look at Nadia before going to shower. I sat on the bench in the shower and just let the water run down my body. I was finally getting back to the old me. Hell, I even had some love for Nadia, but it wasn't like the love I had for Kyn.

I washed my body, then got out. When I walked into the room, Nadia was playing with her pussy, and that shit made me rock up fast. That was so sexy to me.

I made my way to her and wasted no time sliding into her wet, warm pussy. It felt so good, but it was nothing like Kyndall, though. Just as the thought of Kyndall came to my mind, I nutted in Nadia.

Fuck, I needed Kyndall.

"Baby, do you still love me?"

I knew that question was coming sooner or later. The problem was, I didn't really have the answer for her. I cared for her, but I didn't think I could get over what she had done.

"Yea."

She didn't reply, she just rolled over. I didn't know what she expected me to say, but that was all she was going to get from me. It didn't take her long to fall asleep, so I just laid there, staring at the ceiling.

I was ready to meet my son. That was going to be the highlight of my life. The only thing missing was Kyndall. I wished she would just call me. I wanted to know she was OK. I hoped she didn't think I had given up on her. I had been hounding Mom-Mom Ella, but she wasn't giving in. Her birthday was coming up, and I prayed she would be back by then.

I wished that I would have listened back in the day when my dad used to tell me that Kyndall liked me. If I had then, I wouldn't be going through this. I would be happily married to the love of my life.

Even though I had agreed to try and make things work with Nadia, a part of me would never be able to get over the fact that she had fucked my best friend. Then, knowing that she was fucking two other niggas made me wonder how many others she was fucking.

Nadia

I laid in the bed, wide awake, although Cash thought I was sleep. I was doing my best not to be sad. I wanted this man to love me, and he just wouldn't. I should have listened to Mrs. Lucille and just left well enough alone. I wanted to say something about earlier, but I knew it would be like beating a dead horse. They were his family, and I was secondary in his life. He could tell me all day that he wasn't going to kill me, but I knew that was a lie. I was just filling the void in his heart until Kyndall decided to come back. I couldn't lie and say I wasn't enjoying it. He had been so attentive. No matter what I wanted, he made sure I got it. He had even bought me a new truck. Outside of the shit today, we had been good, and that was just how I wanted it to stay.

I rolled over and saw that he was still awake, looking at the ceiling. I slid under the cover and licked the tip of his dick, causing it to rise. I used my tongue to massage the top of his dick just the way he liked. Cash liked to give eye contact while he was getting special attention, so he removed the covers from my head. He palmed the back of my head and continued to fuck my face in a fast motion. The way his body began to tense up, I knew he was about to bust a nut. Once Cash reached his peak, he pulled out of my mouth. Since I was pregnant, he wouldn't let me swallow his nut.

"Damn, girl!" Cash said while trying to catch his breath. Since we were lying here, not talking, I decided to ask questions about the baby.

"Cash, when are you going to do the nursery?"

"I figured we can go house hunting tomorrow."

"What do you mean? I thought you wanted me to live here with you?" I asked because he had asked me to live with him, but I said no, I would just stay at the house with Mrs. Lucille. Ever since that night we ate dinner at his parents' house, we had been staying at his house. Cash was really giving me hope of us getting back together, but the way things had gone down at Shawnee's house today told me everything I needed to know. Then, when I asked him if he loved me, he hesitated to answer, then gave me a dry-ass yes. Now this shit with the house.

"Come on, ma, I told you what the deal was."

"No, Cash, you really haven't told me shit. Let me know what this really is. I'm good enough for you to fuck and lay up underneath, but I'm not good enough for anything else? You're sending me all types of mixed messages, Cashmere. You should have just left me back at the house with Mrs. Lucille because I was just getting over your black ass," I fussed while getting up out the bed. I walked straight into the bathroom to take care of my hygiene, so I could get the fuck out of here. A half hour had passed, and I was now fully dressed and ready to go.

"Nadia, where the fuck you going?"

"I'm going home, Cash. I can't keep doing this with you. I'll call you when I'm ready to have Junior." Yeah, we had decided to name our son Cashmere Whitfield Jr.

"Come on, ma. You're almost nine months pregnant, you don't need to be driving around."

"Cash, I'll be fine. The house is not far from here. I'll text you when I get there." He sucked his teeth and got up and started throwing his clothes on.

"At least let me follow you to make sure you get there safe since you not tryna listen to me, with ya hardheaded ass." I rolled my eyes, then headed downstairs to wait for him. While I waited, I decided to call Mrs. Lucille to let her know I was on my way. Of course, she cursed me out for not waiting until the morning, but I assured her that Cash was going to make sure I got there safe.

Chapter twelve

Keem

I was sitting here, staring at the walls, high as a kite. See, when I had gotten shot months ago, I inherited a pill-popping problem. All I did was pop pills and lay around the house, waiting for Chrissy's ass to come in. She thought I was stupid, but I knew her ass was messing with someone else. She kept me high and my dick empty, so that was the only reason I kept her around. The crazy part was, this bitch had messed up my whole marriage, and she was out here being a hoe.

"Are you hungry? I brought you some Burger King," Chrissy asked while taking me out of my thoughts. I waited until she set the food up directly in front of me to sling it across the room.

"Where the fuck have you been?" I barked.

"Keem, I had to run some errands, and then I had a doctor's appointment."

"Did you bring my pills for me?"

"Keem, you have to eat, baby. That's all you wanna do is pop pills." I slapped her right across her face.

"Chrissy, just give me the fucking pills before I beat ya ass." She threw the pills at me and ran upstairs. Chrissy was getting big, but she wasn't as big as she should have been. See, she had told me she was pregnant right after Neveah was born, but Chrissy looked like she was about four or five months, which meant she had lied so she could keep me around, knowing I was in a vulnerable state, and I would do anything to have a baby. The stupid bitch had lied to me, so guess what? Since she had ruined my life, I ran her ragged and beat her ass when she didn't do what I wanted. Money was getting scarce around here, and I was now working on my savings account. Not only that, but the bills were running up my ass. My whole life had been falling apart ever since I had run out on my wife. I needed to use the bathroom, so I ran upstairs. Hearing Chrissy trying to whisper, I needed to know who her hoe ass was talking to. Once I finished peeing, I ran back in the hall, hoping I hadn't missed the whole conversation.

"Keys, I'll try to come see you, I promise. I love you too." When I heard that shit, I lost it. I ran into the room, grabbed her by her hair and dragged her out of the room.

"So you in my crib, telling other niggas you love them?"

"Keem, I'm sorry, you're hurting me."

"That's the point, you stupid-ass bitch. You fucked my whole marriage up and you out here doing you?" Not caring that she was carrying a baby, I hit her ass over and over again until I was out of breath. She got up off the floor and ran to the bathroom, I guess to clean herself up. Once she was straight, she came out the bathroom with a black eye and busted lip.

"Keem, you can't keep doing this to me. What if you make me lose the baby? Don't you care about the safety of our baby?"

"Bitch, fuck you and that baby. It probably ain't mine anyway," I barked, and she ran off crying, but I didn't give a fuck. She knew good and damn well that baby had a chance of not being mine since she was walking around with community pussy. I know y'all are thinking, what has gotten into me. Well, for starters, my wife had never come back, and all I was left with was Chrissy's nagging ass. Chrissy came walking down the steps with a suitcase from upstairs. I didn't know where she thought she was going. She had created this monster, so she needed to deal with it.

"I'm just going to leave since you act like you don't want me here anyway."

"Chrissy, take ya simple ass back upstairs before I fucking beat the shit out of you again. Kyndall fucking left me! Ain't that what you wanted? You got ya man all to yourself, so get ya ass upstairs and take a shower, then get in the bed and wait for your dick to come upstairs. You wanted all of me, now you got me. I'm the man you love and wanna spend the rest of ya life with, remember? Or, you don't want me anymore because I don't belong to somebody else?" I yelled while giving her a sinister laugh. Chrissy wasn't getting out of this relationship with me unless Kyndall came back to me, and I knew Kyndall was done with me so that just meant Chrissy was stuck with me. After I was done popping a couple of pills, I headed upstairs to fuck the shit out of Chrissy until my dick got tired.

Chrissy

I had been in so much pain since the other day when Keem had fucked me up. He had changed for the worst and had become my worst nightmare. Day after day, I wished

Kyndall would come walking through the door, so that way, he wouldn't want me anymore. My face had cleared up, and Keem let me out of the house because he needed some more pills. While I was out, I was going by Keys since he'd been begging to see me. I had grown to love Keys, but me dealing with Keem stopped me from pursuing anything with Keys. I knocked on his door, and he opened it. The minute he saw me, he pulled me in for a hug and a kiss. Truth be told, I wanted to fuck him, but my body was in so much pain.

"What's wrong? Why you hissed when I pulled you in for a hug?"

"Nothing, this baby has got my body going through changes," I assured him, but I didn't think he bought it.

"Chrissy, you really be thinking I'm stupid. That nigga better not be putting his hands on you while you carrying my seed." While we engaged in a conversation, there was a knock at the door. As soon as Keys opened the door, I wasn't expecting to see her.

"Well, look who it is, just the person I've been trying to get with for months."

"Hello, Reneé, how are you?"

"Bitch, don't how are you me? Word on the streets is, you had something to do with my husband's death, and you better hope and pray that's not true because if it is, I will kill you and that unborn child. We couldn't even give him a proper burial because no body was found."

"Come on, Reneé, that's his sister. Why would she have something to do with it? What brings you by anyway?"

"Keys, I ain't trying to hear shit you saying right now. I came here to see if you could give me some money. Bills are piling up, and money is running low, and you told Dre you would help me with the kids if something were to ever happen to him."

"I know what I said, and I meant what I said. I'll be right back, and behave, Reneé."

"I'm good, Keys, just hurry the hell up."

"I have nothing to do with what happened to my brother, so please stop saying that shit."

"Listen, bitch, ya face ain't pregnant, so watch how you talk to me," she said with so much anger in her voice. I rolled my eyes and headed up to Keys' bedroom. When I made it to his room, he was closing his safe.

"What's wrong, ma? You good?"

"Yes, just a little tired, that's all."

"Well, take ya clothes off and lay down." The way I felt, I might take him up on his offer. I started to pull my pants down and remembered all the bruises I had on my legs and arms. Keys couldn't see that, so I decided against taking my clothes off. Before I got the chance to pull them back up, he walked back into the room.

"Chrissy, what the fuck, man?" he snapped. My head dropped like I was a small child who had done something wrong.

"Calm down, Keys, it's nothing. Don't worry, I'll be OK," I tried to assure him.

"Chrissy, I'm not gon' sit here and argue with you about this nigga because you won't leave him alone. If something happens to my baby, I'm killing both of y'all, and I ain't telling you that shit again. Now take those fucking clothes off and lay down," Keys barked. I never wanted to believe this baby was Keys, but when I found out how far along I was, I knew it was his and not Keem's. When things started getting crazy between Keem and me, I started leaning towards Keys. Yeah, I loved Keem, and I wanted him bad as hell, but I couldn't deal with the man he had become. After the beating he had given me last night, I felt like it was my last night going over there. I wasn't going to lie, though, that look in his eyes when he was high scared the hell out of me. Not only did he beat me, but he also made me have sex with him when I was not in the mood. I was so scared for my life and the baby's life, but I still didn't want Keys to kill him because I was partially the reason his life was all fucked up.

Once I stripped out of my clothes, I climbed into the bed under Keys' big comforter.

"Keys, I'm hungry."

"Ya ass always hungry. Give me a second, and I'll go get you something." He walked out the room for a minute, and my phone started alerting me that I had a text message.

Keem: You think this shit is a game.

Me: Baby, what are you talking about?

Keem: Chrissy, don't play with me.

Me: Keem, I'm not playing.

Keem: *When you leave that nigga's house, you better have some pills or some money to get some.*

After that last text, I didn't even respond. This nigga must have been following me, which was a shock to me because Keem never left the house. Keys must have noticed the scared look on my face when he came back into the room.

"You good, mama?"

"Yes, I'm good, handsome, just hungry, tired and in pain."

"All right, well, take a nap and I'ma go out and get you something."

"No, please stay with me. I want you to hold me. Can't you just order out, please?" He gave me a strange look, but he did as I asked.

"OK, we can order out. Are you sure you're good?"

"Yes, I'm sure, I just miss you and don't want to be alone." Shit, my ass was scared that Keem was outside, and if Keys left, he would come in here and beat my ass. Of course, he would have a lot of balls to do some shit like that, but hell, we were talking about Keem, and he was not in his right state of mind right now.

Keys called and ordered me a steak stromboli from Temple's with onions, peppers, mushrooms, and pepperoni, then he climbed into the bed with me and held me just like I had asked.

Chapter thirteen

Luke

Life had been going great, and all my favorite girls were extremely happy. Shawnee had her house, Joi had just had an amazing birthday party, and my mama was just happy I was happy. Cash was starting to get his head back in the game, so that had taken a lot of work off my plate, but he still hadn't gotten anyone to handle Keem's job. We were actually doing fine without any new people, so I told him to leave it the way it was. We did have to get somebody to handle Dre's spot, but that wasn't about nothing, being as though there were always young soldiers trying to move up in the game.

I was up early, so I decided to go handle my business before Joi and Shawnee woke up. I went by all the traps and made sure the money was straight. I even went to the warehouse to make sure everything was straight, then I had our boy Jake make sure the right money was coming into all the pharmacies. Once that was good, I decided to stop at a Rite Aid and grab a pregnancy test for Shawnee. I kept telling her little ass to go to the doctor, but she kept telling me she was fine. I wasn't about to play with her ass; she was peeing on this stick today. After I got the test, I headed to IHOP and grabbed us all breakfast to go, then went home. After turning a twenty-minute drive into a ten-minute drive, I was now pulling up to my house. I grabbed everything I had and closed the car door, and before I made it to the door, Shawnee opened it.

"Where you go? I woke up looking for you." I shook my head and smiled because she had become really clingy, just like Joi.

"I had to go handle some business, and I didn't wanna wake you." She held the door for me while I came in with a bunch of stuff in my hand.

"What did you get to eat? I'm hungry."

"I got some pancakes, eggs, and bacon for us. I need you to do me a favor before you eat, though."

"Anything for my man." I knew when I pulled the test out the bag, she was going to look at me all crazy. I pulled it out and handed it to her.

"Luke, what do I need this for? I am not pregnant."

"Come on, ma, don't insult my intelligence. Go pee on that stick. You've been running around here for a couple of months now, not feeling good and shit. The minute I say something about the doctor, you tell me you're good. We fucking like teenagers and ya ass ain't had a period in a minute, so go do what I said so we can set you up an appointment." She put her head down and headed to the bathroom. Everything I said was true; not to mention how extra good that pussy felt. Pregnant pussy was definitely the best pussy. While she went to do that, I put her food in the microwave because I knew she was going to want to eat as soon as she got done. After I got finished heating up her food and poured her a glass of orange juice, I headed to see what was taking her so long. When I made it to the bathroom, she was sitting on the toilet, crying.

"Baby, what you in here crying for?"

"Luke, it's too soon for us to have a baby. We just started out months ago." I looked at her with a side-eye. Shawnee was good and tripping right now.

"Shawn, don't play with me, mama. I told you we in this thing forever, so what you talking about? If we good enough to be fucking without using protection, we can be parents. We ain't little kids, and I ain't no lame-ass nigga, so if we gon' be parents, then that's what it's gon' be. Now get yourself together and come feed my baby," I said while bending down to kiss her forehead. Nothing else needed to be said, so I left out to go wake Joi up to eat. When I made it to her room, she was lying there so peacefully.

"Joi," I whispered in her ear.

"What, daddy? I'm tryna sleep." I shook my head and laughed.

"Guess what Daddy got for you?" She jumped up, and her eyes lit up. This little girl stayed getting gifts, so that was all she wanted.

"What did you get me, daddy?" she said with so much excitement.

"Some pancakes."

"Yayyyyyyy, panacakes." The way she said pancakes always made me laugh.

"Come, let's go wash ya face and brush that stinky mouth."

"Where is Nee-Nee?"

"She's already downstairs waiting for you." Joi jumped up and ran to her bathroom to get herself together. After she brushed her teeth and wiped her face, we headed downstairs to join Shawnee. Shawnee was still sitting there like she was in her feelings, and we were going to talk about this when we were done eating. Well, when Joi and I got finished because Shawnee had demolished that food.

"Nee-Nee, where is your food?" Joi asked.

"I ate it, baby. My stomach was growling too much."

"Oh OK, are you still going to sit here with Daddy and me while we eat?"

"Yes, I'll still sit here. How did you sleep last night?"

"Ummm, OK. I had a dream that I went to Walmart and got some new Barbies."

"Joi, you really had a dream, or you wanna go to Walmart and get some new Barbies?" I asked while laughing.

"No, it was really a dream, Daddy."

"I'm glad it was because you don't need anything else right now," I assured her. She poked her lips out, and Shawnee was about to say something, and I cut her right off. Joi didn't need another thing, so we weren't going to get a got damn Barbie today. Shawnee's ass had already bought her a fucking iPhone 8. Like, what five-year-old had a whole iPhone? Hell, a fucking phone period. I was against the whole phone thing, but Meia had gotten her one so she wouldn't play with hers all the time.

Speaking of Meia, I hadn't seen her ass in a minute. I knew if I really wanted to find her, I could, but I wasn't worried about her ass right now. She would just bring headaches and drama to my life, and we were doing well right now. Those drugs and a man must have her occupied to the point she didn't even call for Joi anymore. The thoughts about how she'd been acting lately pissed me off, but I'd deal with that coke whore real soon. After we were finished, we decided to cuddle up on the couch and watch TV. These two were definitely the highlights of my life.

Meia

I hadn't seen my daughter for months due to my drug habit. I didn't want Luke to see me like this, even though I knew he knew already. Shit, Luke was big time, and the streets talked. Money was no longer coming in, and Tory wouldn't give me any. All he would do was feed me and buy me clothes. Of course, he would give me drugs because we got high together, but anything extra I wanted, I had to get on my own. I was only allowed to get high when he did, and that drove me crazy. I wanted my own shit sometimes; I didn't want to share.

"Meia, it's been months, and you still haven't made up your mind about the plan." I didn't want to do this, but Tory kept pressuring me. I wish I would have never bragged about Luke to him.

"Tory, just give me a little more time, please. They moved, and I have to figure out where they live now. I can't just call and ask him for her. He will never let her come, especially after I stole her necklace."

"There are ways to do the shit, Meia, I just think you don't wanna do it. What, you still love that nigga?" I hurried and moved out of his reach because I knew a hit was coming. I didn't feel like fighting his ass today. At first, he would just smack me and yoke me up, but now, he tried to deliver punches and kicks. One thing about me was, I wasn't a punk, so I kindly hit his ass back. So, there had been plenty of nights when we were in this bitch fighting.

"Tory, please don't start. What the fuck does loving him have to do with it? If anything, I'm worried about the welfare of my daughter."

"Bitch, you don't care about that little girl, because if you did, you would have her little ass here with you." Hearing him say that crushed my little heart. I loved Joi with all my heart, I was just in a fucked-up situation right now.

"You know what, fuck you, Tory," I barked while throwing one of my shoes and hitting his stupid ass in the head.

"Meia, don't start throwing shit if you don't want to get fucked up in here."

"Nigga, you ain't fucking me up. Now go on ahead somewhere and leave me alone. I don't feel like being bothered." Tory and I were the craziest couple.

"Meia, did you forget you in my fucking house?"

"Tory, I can leave this fucking rat shack and go to my mama's. You act like I have to be here with your half-ass nickel and diming self. I'm ready to leave and go find me a baller. Ain't no real money being made in here."

"Go ahead and take your crackhead ass somewhere. Don't no baller want a crackhead-ass bitch." Thank God, I was already showered, so I threw some clothes on and headed out the door. I decided to go pass Luke's mom's house since I didn't know where his new home was. I had to get myself prepared to feel Luke's wrath. I knew when he saw me, he was going to kick my ass for taking Joi's necklace. After putting my shoes on, I grabbed my phone, keys, and purse and walked out the door. I jumped in my car and peeled off. Fifteen minutes went by, and I was now pulling up to Luke's mom's house. Her car was parked out in the front, so I knew she was here. No one else's car was here, so I was glad she was alone. I had to go in here and lay it on thick. I knocked on the door a couple of times before she opened it.

"Hey, mama," I spoke as soon as the door opened.

"Hey, Meia, what you doing here?"

"Mama, I wanted to know if I can come in and talk to you."

"Sure, come on in. What's wrong with you, baby? You sick?"

"I'm OK, just been a little stressed since Luke won't let me see Joi."

"Well, Meia, you haven't been the best mother these past few months. Don't you think he has a reason to feel the way he's been feeling? Then my grandbaby running around telling everybody her mom stole her necklace so she wants a new mom. That shit is not right, Meia. I wanted to come kick ya ass myself. If you need help, then just let us know; you never had to steal from Luke. Then, of all things, you take something from Joi. What the fuck were you thinking?"

"I know, Mama, and I'm so sorry. I'm trying to make things right and get help, so Luke will let me keep Joi again."

"Well, have you talked to him?"

"No, he won't answer any of my phone calls. In a couple of weeks, I plan on going to rehab. Can you do me a favor and get Joi over here so I can see her?"

"Meia, now you know I don't get in y'all's business."

"I know, Mama, but I need to see Joi before I go so I can stay focused and remember what I'm doing this for. Missing her like this has me so stressed."

"All right, I'll see what I can do, but if you fuck this up, I'll never help you again, Meia. You know Luke is my heart, and I would die if he stops talking to me behind you." I knew she would give in if I said something about getting help. Tory was going to be excited when he finds out that I figured out how to get the plan in motion. Mama and I sat and talked for a while, and she told me how mad she was that I had missed Joi's birthday. I was kind of mad at myself, but I knew I couldn't step foot in that house. Luke, Cash, and that crazy-ass girlfriend Luke has would have kicked my ass. Once we wrapped up our conversation, I made Mama promise not to tell Luke anything about me getting help. I didn't want him to know she and I had any contact because I knew he would tell her not to talk to me.

Chapter Fourteen

Kyndall

It had been a week since I had gotten the surgery done. The doctor didn't want me on my feet, but I was tired of sitting in this damn house. All I wanted was some good-ass wings, so I was going to go out to eat, then make my way back in the house. Before I went out, I needed to contact Mom-Mom Ella, so I dialed her number, and she picked up on the first ring.

"Hey, Mom-Mom, what you doing?"

"Hey, baby. Nothing, sitting here watching my *Law & Order* reruns. What you doing? Have you been resting like the doctor said?"

"Yeah, I have, but I'm sick of being in this damn house, Mom-Mom."

"Kyndall, you better listen to the doctor's orders."

"I am, Mom-Mom, and Danni has been a drill sergeant."

"That's good. She is exactly what your hard headed ass needs." I laughed at my Mom-Mom because she was hilarious at times. When I called and told her what the doctor had told me and how my chances of finally carrying a baby full term were high, she was excited for me, and we both cried on the phone.

"How's Shawnee doing?"

"She's doing great. That boy don' bought her this big-ass house that she doesn't even need. Hell, her ass ain't even been going out of town for work. Luke came along and shut shit down. She needed that because I thought she was gon' end up being a little bitter-ass, lonely girl."

"Mom-Mom, she was never bitter."

"Yes the hell she was. That's why her attitude always stayed on one. She needed some on-the-regular penis." I was on the floor, cracking up.

"Mom-Mom, I ain't about to play with you today."

"When are you going to tell Cash about the baby, Kyndall?" I knew that question was coming. I just held the phone. "I know you hear me talking to you, girl."

"I'm not ready for that, Mom-Mom."

"Kyndall, I don't care what you're ready for. Him not seeing your belly grow, feeling the movement, and going through all the things you go through in pregnancy isn't fair, baby. Then, God forbid if something happens and he's not there to help you go through it."

"Mom-Mom, I have to go," I said right before I disconnected our call. I knew she was going to be pissed with me, but I didn't care. That was just something I wasn't ready for.

Pulling out my phone, I looked up Buffalo Wild Wings. I had a taste for a variety of wings, so that was where I was going. I thanked God there was one not far from Danni's house. Throwing on a grey sweater dress and my grey UGGS, I was good and comfortable. Since Danni knew I was pregnant, I was so glad I didn't have to cover up with big-ass t-shirts and hoodies. Once I was ready, I grabbed my bag and headed out. Danni was on a date so she couldn't stop me. The thought of the wings had my mouth watering.

In ten minutes, I was pulling into the parking lot. As soon as I found a parking space, I parked, then turned the car off and nearly ran into the restaurant. Once I made it through the door, the greeter showed me to my table since I was alone.

"Can I get you a drink?"

"Yes, please give me your biggest Sprite." I knew damn well I wasn't supposed to be drinking soda, but I was going to enjoy this meal.

"OK, Sprite coming right up. Do you need a couple of minutes, or do you know what you want already?"

"I'm ready to order. I want an order of the fried pickles, roasted garlic mushrooms, and an order of parmesan garlic wings."

"Bone in or out?" she asked.

"Bone in, please and thank you."

"All right, your Sprite will be right out, and your order shortly after." As soon as she walked away, I stood up to take my jacket off. I needed to get comfortable to dig into this food.

I didn't realize I was still standing up until I heard a voice I hadn't heard in a year.

"Kyndall, is that you?" he asked. I dropped my head like a kid who had been caught in the cookie jar. I raised it slowly because I felt him standing there, staring at me.

"Hey, Mr. Carson," I mumbled. He gave me a weird look, so I knew he was going to call Cash as soon as he walked off.

"Hey, baby, how have you been? I see you're expecting. Congratulations, honey." Forgetting all about my belly, I grabbed it and gave him a half-smile.

"Thank you so much, Mr. Carson, and it was nice seeing you," I said, hoping he would get the picture that I didn't want to talk anymore.

"All right, Kyndall, I'll be down here on business for a little while, so maybe we will run into each other again. I'll be sure to tell Della I saw you. You know how she feels about you."

"OK, Mr. Carson. Tell her I said hello." It was weird that he only said he was going to tell his wife I said hello and not Cash. Yeah, he knew the whole story, and as soon as he left, he was calling Cash. I didn't have an appetite any longer, so I asked the waitress to bag my food up, and I headed home. That was why I should have stayed my hard headed ass in the house.

Shawnee

I had found out I was pregnant two weeks ago, and Luke had been under my ass since. I mean, he was always at home. Normally, he would have been hanging with Cash, but he had yet to do that. Hell, I liked my damn alone time. This nigga even went to the nail shop with Joi and me. I needed some fucking me time. Luke was on the phone with his mom, so I headed to my office so I could get these sketches done for this dress I was doing for some lady in Cali. She was set to come and view them in three days, so I knew I needed to get them done. My business was just starting to pick back up again. Shit, all the chilling I'd been doing since I had met Luke, it felt like I didn't have a damn job, but the way my account looked, you knew good and got damn well I had a job. Luke had handled everything since we'd been together, so my money was my money.

"Hey, baby. What are you doing?" Luke asked as he sat on the couch that was in my office.

"Nothing, working on a dress I should have had done a week ago. I'm just so tired, all I wanna do is lay in bed."

"Well, just take a break or hire someone to help you, that way it won't be too much on you. Or maybe you need to get a building and hire a whole team. As a matter of fact, gon' call ol' girl and have her find you a building." I just shook my head because he swore he was running shit, when in reality, he didn't run his own damn bath water.

"OK, baby, I will do it when I get done with this. Where my baby girl?"

"I just made her take a nap. She has been up all day, and she was starting to do shit she knew she didn't need to be doing," he fussed. I prayed I would have a boy because he was so hard on Joi. I felt bad for her sometimes, because most times, she was just being a kid.

"OK. What you want for dinner?" I asked.

"Pasta," he smiled. That made me think of Kyndall. I missed her like crazy. I knew she was OK, but I couldn't help but miss her crazy ass. Every time I thought about her being gone, I got sad because I knew she would still be hurt when she came back and found out that Nadia was having Cash's baby. That was part of the reason I hadn't gone and got her ass myself.

"OK. I will go down and cook in a sec. Have you talked to your mom? She keeps calling, asking to get Joi."

"Yea, I talked to her, but something is not right. She has never done that. Normally, she would just wait until we brought her." Luke was so paranoid. He always thought somebody was being a snake. I will say that most times he was right, but this was his mom we were talking about. She loved Joi just as much as we did, so I didn't think she would do anything that would put Joi in harm's way.

"I think you should let her go. That way, we can fuck and actually enjoy it. Hell, I feel like I'm living with Mom-Mom Ella. I'm starting to think she has cameras or something in the house," I laughed. He knew I was right, so he laughed with me.

"OK, I will take her in the morning before we go to the doctor. When are we gon' tell her about the baby?"

"I don't know, maybe once she comes back from your mom's house," I told him as I finished up what I was doing. I didn't think I had ever taken this long to do a sketch. She had changed her mind so many times, I guess she thought she was the only client I had.

"Well, I'm going to cook," I said, getting up. I made sure I got up so Luke could see the boy shorts I was wearing. I knew I had gotten his attention when he grabbed his dick.

"Come here," he demanded. I did as I was told and made my way over to him. He pulled his dick out and my mouth watered. This man had the prettiest damn dick I had ever seen. I locked the door to my office and dropped to my knees. Joi was just going to have to wait today. I needed a good, long nut.

I took him into my mouth, and that nigga damn near ran up the damn wall. "What you doing, baby?" he moaned. I knew I had him right there. I put the rest of him in my mouth and started moving my tongue around. He was ready to nut, but I wasn't having that. I pulled him out of my mouth and straddled him. I wanted to scream out when I felt the pressure of his dick head pressing against my opening. For the life of me, I couldn't understand how it always felt like this. After a few minutes, I was riding him like my life depended on it. I guess he felt I was taking over because he flipped me over without pulling out. I didn't even think that was possible.

"Shit, baby," I moaned. This was the most satisfying pain I had ever been through.

"Just like that, Shawn, baby. Throw that ass back for Daddy," he instructed. I was doing what I was told when I heard a little knock on the door.

"Mommy," Joi called out.

"Hold on, baby, Mommy's cummin'." We both laughed as we got our nuts. After I pulled my panties back up, Luke went next to the other door, so he could go out as Joi came in.

"Hey, Mommy's baby," I said, opening the door so she could come in.

"I had a nightmare, and I want you to come sleep with me." She grabbed my hand and led me to me and Luke's room. When we made it in the room, Luke was in the shower. We both got in the bed, and before I knew it, we had drifted off to sleep.

Chapter fifteen

Luke

Since Shawnee and Joi were asleep, I decided I would get out and kick it with the guys for a while. After I made sure they were good, I headed out. I knew Cash was probably at this building he was getting ready to fix and make a strip club. Once I called him and confirmed that, I was headed that way.

As soon as I pulled up, I jumped out. I felt like I was missing my nigga. Ever since we had found out we were pregnant, I had been at home. I was happy as hell that she was pregnant because I had been trying since the first time we fucked.

"Damn, nigga, Shawnee let you out the house," Cash joked.

"I'm grown, don't nobody let me do shit," I countered back.

"Well, let's call my sis and ask her what she thinks about this." That nigga was for real dialing her, and I snatched that nigga's phone so fast.

"You lost yo' damn mind." I knew she didn't play, and so did he, so I didn't know why he was playing like that.

"What's been good with you, though?" I asked since we hadn't really seen each other. The most he did was check on Joi and Shawnee.

"Shit really. Nadia about to bust any day now. The pharmacy is still doing good, thanks to you. Hopefully, I will have this club open in the next couple of months. Shit,

I'm just looking for a way out. It's almost time for us to pass this shit on to someone else and sit back and enjoy life. What's happening in your life?"

"Sounds good to me. I'm working on some barber shops right now, and I'm looking for a building for Shawnee. Oh, yea, and a nigga finna have a junior," I told him, beaming. I was happy as hell about me and Shawnee's baby.

"Damn, that's what's up. Can a nigga be the goddaddy?" he asked. I pushed that nigga because he knew better than to ask some shit like that.

"That shouldn't have been a question, nigga. Ain't you Joi's god daddy? Everything I produce is going to be your godchild. You know damn well I don't fuck with nobody but you," I replied as I lit the blunt I had behind my ear.

"All I'm missing is Kyndall. I just wish I could see her. Hell, just hearing her voice would be good for me." He looked sad as hell. I didn't know where Kyndall was, but I did know that Shawnee had a way of checking on her, I just wasn't going to be the one to tell him that. He was finally back to the old Cash, and I wanted him to stay that way. I knew that if the thought of Kyndall coming back came to his mind, then he was going to spazz, and I didn't have time for that bullshit.

"Have you heard from Keem's bitch ass?" I asked. I couldn't lie, I just knew Cash was going to go and finish his ass off. If it had been me, his ass would have been floating in a river right now. I guess he had let him live because he had fucked that nigga's wife.

"Hell naw. I want to kill his ass, but I know Kyndall will hate my ass more than she already does."

"Nigga, trust me, she doesn't hate yo' ass. She loves you. She will be back soon. The question is, what are you going to do about Nadia when she comes back? You know Kyndall is going to beat her ass." We both laughed because Kyndall was so mellow. Shawnee told me that Kyndall used to beat ass back when they were in high school, but I couldn't see Kyndall like that.

"We will cross that bridge when we get there. Nadia was all in her feelings the other day and called herself moving out."

"Y'all crazy as hell," I told him as I pulled off the blunt we were smoking. It felt good to be kicking it with my bro. We used to do this shit on a daily before I met Shawnee.

Cash was the only nigga I could say I truly trusted. I had several niggas I had grown up with that I was cool with, but Cash was like my brother. I trusted him with my life. The last time I was close to someone like this, he stole from me, and that shit had scarred me, for real. I didn't have to worry about that with Cash because he had his own money. Hell, he was putting money in my pocket.

We talked and smoked for what seemed like hours. I looked at my phone and Shawnee was calling, so I knew it was time for me to take my ass home. We said our goodbyes and went our separate ways.

As soon as I got back in the car, I called her back so I could see if she wanted me to stop and get anything.

"Baby, you been gone forever. We miss you," she whined as soon as she answered. I just laughed. She was being extra as hell.

"I'm on my way to y'all now, baby," I assured her. I knew she was going to ask how far I was, so I beat her to it. "I'm like ten minutes away. Make sure Joi is in her bed because I'm finna get some of that wet pussy when I get there."

"OK, baby, hurry up," was all she said before ending the call. I would have never thought I would have been in love like this. I loved Meia, but there was nothing like the love I had for Shawnee. Shawnee was different. She wasn't there for the money and the street fame. She loved me for me, and that was some shit you didn't see often. Then, to top that, she had her own money. Most females didn't have shit to offer but some pussy. Not to mention how she loved Joi like she was her own. She was the whole package.

I pulled into my gate and shut my car off, then used my key to unlock the door. When I walked in, I got the surprise of my life. She was lying on the couch, ass naked. My dick was so hard, it felt like it was going to burst through my pants.

"Damn, baby. That's all mine?" I asked, even though I knew the answer. She nodded her head, but that wasn't enough for me. I needed to hear her say it. I made my way over to her and slipped my finger into her opening. "I'm going to ask one more time, is this all mine?"

"Mmmm, yesssss, daddy," she moaned. She was loud as hell, so I looked towards the stairs because I knew Joi was coming.

"She's knocked out. I gave her some Benadryl. She will be out for a while, so come on and have dessert." I jumped in head first. It had been a while since we had been able to make love, and I was ready.

Chrissy

I had been avoiding the hell out of Keem. I knew that whenever he caught up with me, he was going to kick my ass. A part of me wanted to say fuck Keem, but then I felt guilty about how I had pretty much ruined his life. I felt stupid as fuck. I wanted this man so bad, I had told his wife about us. Now that I was getting ready to be a mother, there was a lot I regretted. I knew I wouldn't want anyone to do my baby like that.

The fucked-up part was, I had now developed feelings for Keys. Keys showed me the kind of love I had searched for my whole life. He never judged me. All he worried about was if I was OK.

Keem, on the other hand, didn't care about shit but getting high. He had been calling me non- stop, but I had been ignoring the calls. He had threatened my life and my baby's life, and that was part of the reason I had been trying to stay away. I was also enjoying being with Keys. I knew that as long as he was around, then Keem wouldn't fuck with me.

I had a doctor's appointment, and Keys wasn't able to go with me, I just prayed I didn't run into Keem.

"Hey, baby. I'm gone, I will see you later," I yelled to him. He was in his little man cave, so I knew he wasn't going to walk me to the door.

"OK, love you, Chris."

"Love you too," I yelled as I walked out the door. When I walked outside, I looked around to be sure it was safe, then I headed to the car. It took me no time to get to the doctor's office. When I pulled in the lot, I got a funny feeling, but I brushed it off. I made my way into the building as fast as I could. I wanted to make sure I was in the open, so if he did pop up, someone would see what was going on. I felt so relieved when I sat down in the doctor's office. I was able to breathe.

They called me to the back and did the normal check up on me. When all of that was done, I set my next appointment, then I headed back to the car. I felt relaxed because two ladies were walking in front of me. I was looking through my phone when I felt someone grab me. I knew who it was.

"So you really thought I was going to let you get away that easy? I told you before that you wanted me, so now you got me. If you had just stayed in your lane, and wouldn't have told my wife about us, then we would be OK," he said, pulling me towards his car. I couldn't blame anyone but myself. I had brought this on myself.

"Keem, please," I cried.

"Bitch, if you scream, I will kick you right in your fucking stomach. I don't even know why the fuck you're crying now," he said as we made it to his car. His car was parked behind the doctor's office where no one could hear or see me. Once we made it to his car, he delivered blow after blow to my face like I was a man. I then fell to the ground, and he delivered a kick to my belly. I was in so much pain all over my body. I felt a warm gush between my legs, and I knew exactly what the fuck was happening.

"Keem, please, you're hurting the baby," I managed to get out.

"Hoe, fuck you and that baby. It's not mine anyway. I guess you think I'm dumb. If that was my baby, it would have been born by now." As soon as the last word left his mouth, he delivered another kick straight to my face, then I blacked out.

****

The beeping sounds woke me up out of my sleep, and the minute I felt my stomach, the tears started to fall. I couldn't see who was in the room with me because my eyes were swollen shut. Keem had really done a number on me.

"Baby, stop crying. I'm here now." I heard Keys' voice and was so happy.

"I'm sorry, Keys. I'm sorry the baby is gone, and it's all my fault."

"Shh, it's not your fault. Stop crying, you've already been through so much. Who did this to you?" I didn't want to tell him, but then I thought, fuck Keem. He had taken my baby's life, and now his would be taken.

"Hakeem did it. He was upset with me because I was going to tell you and Tory that he killed Dre." I knew I had lied, but I wanted to add more fuel to the fire. Keys sat for a second before he said anything.

"All right, I'm going to handle his ass, but when the cops ask you what happened, say you don't remember anything. Also, tell them you don't know who would have a vendetta against you. I wanna handle him myself, and I can't have any cops getting in my way."

"OK, Keys, but I'm still sorry about the baby."

"Chris, baby, don't worry about it. The doctors said you'll be able to have more kids, so when you get well, we will try again." I felt like shit for everything that had gone down, but I had definitely learned my lesson. From now on, I was changing my life, and I didn't want anybody else's man. I had Keys, and it was about time I stopped playing with him and made it official.

Chapter sixteen

Keem

I had taken a drive right outside of Jersey until things died down. I didn't think the nigga Chrissy was with was in the streets like that, so I wasn't worried about him. I was worried about if her hoe ass was going to run to the police. Money was running low, but I still had the cards to a joint account that Kyndall and I had. When I went to the bank, they said it was still active, so I drew half the money out and had it with me. Now I was in an old, beat-down motel room, lying across the bed. There were prostitutes in the front, and drug dealers on the next corner. Everything I needed was right in this area. One of the hookers put me on to a pill supplier, so I had pills on deck. Shorty even said she would be back to keep me company, and I was all for that.

While I was lying there, thoughts of what I had done to Chrissy came to mind, and I laughed. My ass had become crazy as shit over the past couple of months. All the shit that had happened to me, I guess it was taking a toll on me. It was like I had no feelings about anything. Kyndall was once my world, and I had lost her, so there was basically nothing to give a fuck about anymore. There was a knock at the door, and I knew it was the hooker from earlier. I didn't usually do snow bunnies, but baby girl was stacked, and she told me she liked black dick.

"Hey, handsome," she cooed when I opened the door.

"What's up, beautiful? Come on in, I've been waiting for you."

"Were you really?"

"Yes, I was. It's been a little minute since I had some enjoyment in my life."

"Well, I think I can handle that," she said while dropping to her knees, not wasting any time pleasing me. Once she made it to her knees, she started to unbutton my jeans. The minute they were unbuttoned and down to my knees, my mans poked out of my boxers. The minute she saw it, she licked the head like it was a lollipop, before taking me into her mouth. I grabbed a handful of her blonde hair and directed her head as I fucked her face.

"FUCK, GIRL! Suck that shit just like that." I had her head going in a fast motion, then she pulled out, and when she pulled out, spit fell out of her mouth and ran down her chin. That shit turned me on. Baby girl was making it nice and sloppy for me. As soon as I felt the head of my dick hit her tonsils, that was it for me, and I was now busting the first nut of the night. I looked down at her while I shot my seeds down her throat. She smiled at me while wiping her mouth. She got up off her knees, then headed over to the little sofa that was in the room.

"Let me get myself prepared for you, daddy." She pulled out a sandwich bag with white powder in it, then she went back in her bag and grabbed a small mirror and a razor. Once she had everything she needed, she made three straight lines, then snorted two of them quick as hell. She held her head back and started laughing out of the blue. That shit must have been some good shit.

"You good, beautiful?"

"Yeah, I'm great, now that I've gotten my medicine. Would you like to do a line?"

"Nah, I'm good, I got my pills."

"You ain't felt a high until you felt this kind. Pills are cool, but this gets you high much faster. Plus, you'll be able to keep up with me tonight." Shit, I figured why not try it; can't fuck me up any worse than I already am. I walked over to her and snorted the last line she had on the mirror. That shit hit me instantly, and I had to sit down for a second to get my mind right. The feeling my body had was like no other. It was probably because of the pill I had taken not too long ago. The chick stood up while I was still trying to get my mind right and stripped out of her clothes. Baby girl's body was bad as fuck, and nobody could tell me she hadn't paid for that shit. My dick started to brick up, so I did the honors of unleashing the beast once again for her sexy ass. She walked over to me and opened a condom, then slid it on my dick. Once the condom was on, and my dick was ready, she slid on my dick. Her shit wasn't as tight as I would have liked it to be, but I guess I couldn't expect much from a hooker. While she rode my dick, she directed my hand to her asshole, I guessed so I could play with it. So, I did what she wanted, and the minute I started moving my fingers in and out of her asshole, she came good and hard.

"Can you fuck me in my ass with that big cock?" she cooed in my ear. I wasn't a butt man, but her pussy was loose, and I didn't think I would bust that way. I turned her ass around and entered her ass slowly like she had directed me to. This shit felt so fucking good. It was nice, tight, warm, and I felt myself about to cum any minute now. I slowed up again, then started back up.

"FUCK! This shit feels so fucking good."

"This dick feels so good, daddy." While I fucked her in her asshole, she played with her clit, and I rubbed her titties. We were both about to cum any minute. I felt my nut building as I pounded in and out of her ass.

"I'm about to cum!" I yelled like a little bitch.

"Me too, daddy, me too." Five minutes later, she and I came together. We both fell on the couch, breathing rapidly. Once I got my breathing straight, I took the condom off and noticed my dick was still sitting at attention. She looked at me and winked while crawling back over to me. That coke must have had my dick hard because, usually, my dick went soft after I nutted, and I would have to wait a little while before I could get hard again. Once she made it over to me, she took my dick into her mouth once more. I could tell this was going to be a long night for me, but I didn't mind. The good thing about this was, I didn't have to pay her; she wanted me to fuck her for the night, and I didn't mind at all. It had been a minute, and I needed to bust a couple of nuts. Shit, after tonight, I didn't even know where I was headed, but I guessed I would push that to the back of my head for now.

Nadia

Since it was almost time for Junior to make his grand appearance, I had been in my feelings about numerous things. One thing was that my daughter had been on my mind heavy lately. I couldn't believe I had never told Cash anything about her. Knowing how he would feel about this, the tears started to fall down my face.

"What you in here crying for?" Mrs. Lucille came walking into my room. I swear there were cameras in here because this old hag always caught me crying.

"Nothing, I'll be OK, Mrs. Lucille."

"Nadia, don't lie to me. You've been looking down around here all week." I'd talked to her about so many things, so I didn't think telling her about this would be a problem.

"Mrs. Lucille, I have something to tell you, and please don't judge me. Just hear me out, then tell me what you think I should do."

"Nadia, I haven't judged you not one time since you've been here. All I have been doing is getting you going in the right direction."

"OK, well, I have a five-year-old daughter named Nya who my sister took from me when I was sixteen. She's been on my mind a lot lately since I'm about to give birth to Junior. The crazy part about all of this is, my sister is going to feel some type of way because I'm pregnant again." Mrs. Lucille sat there in deep thought before she decided to speak.

"Well, this is some very shocking news, considering I don't ever hear you say anything about your daughter. Does Cash even know about her?" I knew this question was coming.

"I don't talk about her because she was a part of my life I tried to put behind me. See, I was raped, so she is a product of rape. I never even told my sister that part, she just always assumed I was being a hot ass and got pregnant. So, 'I was having this baby since I was being grown,' were her exact words." This was the first time I had ever told anyone about how I had gotten pregnant with Nya. My sister didn't even know. Every time I would try to tell her, she would cut me off and tell me that I was going to be just like our hoe-ass mama, so I just never said anything. I pushed having a kid to the back of my head and went on with my life.

"I understand why you tried to push it to the back of your head, but talking about it may have helped you cope with it better. As far as your little girl, she didn't ask to be here. Yeah, it was a hurtful situation that brought her here, but since you're trying to change your life, you might want to establish some type of relationship with her while she is still small. Now, Cash is going to be a different story. This is something you should have told him the minute y'all started to get serious in your relationship. Girl, you just can't catch a break when it comes to you and Cash. Y'all are just toxic to each other."

"He's gonna hate me again."

"He's going to be mad about you not telling him, but you need to come clean about it. You also need to call your sister and let her know about Junior coming soon. Then maybe after you have him and get settled, y'all can start some type of visitation for Nya. I'll be here for you as much as I can while you're going through all of this. Call your sister while I finish up dinner." I grabbed my phone and dialed Nadeen's number, and she picked up on the second ring.

"Well, hello, Nadia. You finally realized you had a family." I looked at my phone and rolled my ass. She never had anything nice to say, with her simple ass.

"Hey, Nadeen, how are you and Nya doing?"

"We are doing great, but I doubt if you really care. What do you want, Nadia?" I knew she would be pissed with me because it had been months since I had last talked to them, and I said I was going to see if I could make it to see them. Truthfully, it had slipped my mind because of everything I had going on.

"I was calling to let you know that you had a nephew on the way, and he's due any day now. I also wanted you to know that I'm changing my life around, and I wanted Nya to be a part of it." She hadn't said anything yet, but I knew she was about to be a real bitch.

"Congratulations on the baby, and whenever you're ready to start visitation with Nya, just let me know. As long as you're doing good, Nadia, I don't mind you seeing your daughter. When you were younger, you did nothing but show out and get in trouble, then you got pregnant. I was tryna raise you to be the best woman you could be, but you messed up by being grown." I couldn't take it anymore; it was time for me to explain to her why I hadn't come back for Nya when I got of age.

"Nadeen, the reason I didn't come back for Nya when I got of age was because she was a part of my life I was trying to leave in the past. See, Nya was the product of a rape, and that's why I didn't wanna keep her, but you made me. I tried to explain it to you, but all you kept saying was I was a little hot ass, and I was going to end up going down the same road as Mama. YOU NEVER LISTENED TO ME!" I yelled into the phone. I heard sniffling on the other end, and that was when I noticed we were both crying our eyes out.

"Nadia, I'm so sorry, baby. I didn't know. I didn't know," she said in between cries. Junior was doing backflips in my stomach. I guess he didn't like all this crying and yelling I was doing. The movement slowed down, then I felt a sharp pain that caused me to scream.

"Arrrrrgh! Nadeen, I think I need to call you back," I managed to get out.

"Nadia, I'm coming now. Let me call Derrick to let him know." The minute my sister hung up, another pain came. This time, Mrs. Lucille must have heard me because she came running upstairs.

"Are you OK?" she asked, looking nervous.

"No, call Cash, I think it's time."

"All right, come on and let me help you downstairs. Where are the bags?"

"There should be a Gucci duffle bag and a Polo diaper bag sitting in the bottom of the closet." Once we made it downstairs, she went out to start the car while I called Cash. I dialed his number, and he picked up on the first ring.

"What's up, baby mama?" I hated when his simple ass called me that.

"I'm on my way to the hospital, the baby is coming." As soon as those words left my mouth, my water broke. I screamed Mrs. Lucille's name to let her know.

"Baby, what's wrong, are you OK?" Cash asked, concerned.

"Yes, I'm cool, my water just broke, though. I'm getting in the car now, so hurry and get to the hospital."

"I'm already en route, but don't hang up on me. I wanna stay on the phone until you get there." The whole way to the hospital, Cash wanted to stay on the phone, and all I was doing was screaming and breathing heavily. Mrs. Lucille got us to the hospital in fifteen minutes. She left me in the car while she went in to get me a wheelchair. While she was inside, I felt the passenger side door open, and it was Cash. He hadn't told me he was here. *Got me still holding the damn phone.*

"Cash, it hurts so bad," I cried. He lifted me out of the car and carried me inside. I guess Mrs. Lucille was taking too long.

"My girl is having a baby," he barked as soon as he walked in the hospital. Mrs. Lucille walked out with the wheelchair, but the way Cash was acting, they came running with a gurney. Once they placed me on the gurney, they ran me to labor and delivery. They asked me a ton of questions, one being if I had ever given birth. I looked at Cash, and the tears started to fall as I shook my head yes. Cash looked at me and shook his head. I could tell he was pissed, but he told the doctor yes, and answered all the rest of the questions they asked. I was in too much pain to say anything. We made it to labor and delivery, and they hooked me up to all the monitors. The baby's heart was good and strong, his head was in place, and I was already four centimeters, so this labor wouldn't be long at all. Since I was already four centimeters, I figured I might as well go natural. Cash sat quietly, not saying much of anything to me, and I guessed I couldn't blame him. He did hold my hand the whole time because he could see I was in a lot of pain. The pain was starting to get unbearable, but I was trying my hardest not to get the epidural.

"Cash, can you get me some ice chips, please?" He let my hand go and did as I asked. I didn't like the fact that he wasn't talking to me, but I knew he was mad.

"Here goes your ice. Why didn't you get something for pain, baby?"

"I want to go natural."

"But it's hurting you too much."

"I'll be OK, Cash, as soon as our little man makes his grand entrance." Cash kissed my forehead, then sat in the chair next to me, holding my hand while Mrs. Lucille sat in the chair across the room, watching Cash and me.

Two long hours later…

The doctor came in to do the final check, and I was happy when he told his crew it was time. "Ms. Williams, it's time to push," the doctor told me. I had been in pain for hours, and I was so ready for this baby to come out of me. After about twenty minutes, I finally pushed out Cashmere Whitfield Jr., weighing eight pounds, twelve ounces, and twenty inches long. This baby was so damn big and looked just like Cash. He was so happy, and I could see it in his face. I was so exhausted, all I wanted to do was sleep. I loved my baby boy and holding him made me the happiest mother in the world. I couldn't wait to love on him.

"Thank you, Nadia," Cash said while kissing me.

"You're welcome, baby." Mrs. Lucille stood next to Cash while he held the baby, and she smiled.

"You did real good, Nadia, pushing that big-ass turkey out." Cash and I both laughed at her crazy ass.

"Nadia, get some rest. My parents and Luke will be up here later to see the baby." I agreed with Cash; I definitely needed a nap. That labor had worn my ass out. After I made sure Junior was OK, I drifted off to sleep.

Chapter Seventeen

Cash

Nadia had given birth to my pride and joy about four hours ago. Cash Jr. was the spitting image of me, so I knew he was mine. I knew I had told her I believed her, but I had to make sure he was when he made it into this world. I was pissed when the doctor asked if this was her first birth and she said no, but where was the baby? What happened to it? Nadia was keeping something like that from me, and I was pissed, but seeing my junior made me leave it alone for now. My family wanted to come up here, but I asked them to wait until later since Nadia was tired. She was still sleeping, but they were on their way. I was so glad my pops had come back into town last night just for a couple of weeks, then he was going back to Memphis. I was so glad she had the baby before he went back. While I was in the waiting room, waiting for my parents, a lady walked up with a little girl, asking to see Nadia. She looked like her, but I had never met her. I walked over to the desk to ask who she was.

"Hello, I happened to hear you ask for Nadia's room."

"Yes, I'm Nadeen, her sister, and this is her daughter, Nya." My face went straight to the little girl, and yeah, she looked just like Nadia. I wondered why she hadn't told me about her.

"My fault for staring like that, I've just never met any of her family. I'm Cash, the father of the baby she just had."

"Oh, hey, Cash, nice to meet you. How is she? We were on the phone when the pain started, but I had to get a flight from Ohio."

"Oh OK, well, she's doing fine. She's sleeping right now. Cashmere Whitfield Jr. is fine. He weighed eight pounds, twelve ounces, and he is twenty inches long."

"Wow, little man weighed a lot. Can I go up to see her? I haven't seen my sister in about a year."

"You can go up, but can I ask you a question?"

"If it's anything about my sister, I would appreciate it if you ask her yourself. She has her reasons for not telling you about Nya. Was it right, no, but hear her out before you shut her out." I gave her a head nod, and she went on her way, and I sat in the waiting room and waited for my parents. I'd had a long day today and wanted some sleep. I rested my head on the back of the couch and dozed off.

"Wake ya big head ass up," Luke said, waking me out of my sleep.

"Damn, I didn't mean to fall asleep. What took ya ass so damn long?"

"I had to drop Joi off at my mama's house. She told me to tell you congratulations."

"I'll call her later to tell her thank you, but let me tell you how my Jr. came out looking like a damn football player. Already can fit in some clothes and sneaks." Luke burst out laughing.

"Damn, how much did he weigh?"

"Eight pounds, twelve ounces, and he is twenty inches long."

"Damn, Joi only weighed six pounds. Does he look like you?"

"Just like me, man. Ain't no denying him at all, but check this. How she got a daughter she never told me about. Her sister just popped up from Ohio with the little girl. She looks like she's the same age as Joi. I tried to ask her sister about it, and she shut that shit down before I even got to ask the question. Told me to ask Nadia myself, but she also told me she had her reasons and to just hear her out before I cut her off."

"Well, baby girl did have a point. It's not her place to tell you anything about Nadia, and nigga, she doesn't know you, her loyalty lies with her sister."

"Hey, son, congratulations!" my pops said while walking over to Luke and me.

"Old Man Carson, what's good?" Luke spoke.

"Little nigga, what I tell you about calling me old?" he said while pulling Luke in for a hug.

"Hey, my babies!" my mom beamed as she walked up to us. I stood up and pulled her in for a hug, then I hugged my pops. Luke hugged my mom, and we all headed to the nursery to see Junior. Once we made it to the nursery, I asked the nurse to put him at the window so they all could see him.

"OH MY GOD! Cash, look at him, he's so adorable. He looks just like your baby pictures," my mama said with so much excitement.

"You did good, son," my pops said while smiling.

"He is all me. I'm so happy he is healthy. All my family is here for my special day except Kyndall," I thought out loud, and they all looked at me like I was crazy.

"Even if Kyn were around, she would not have stepped foot in this hospital, nigga, and you know that," Luke blurted out before laughing.

"Speaking of Kyndall, I meant to call you a couple of days ago. I saw her in Memphis, sitting at a wing spot all alone, and she's pregnant."

"Say what now, pops?" My dad had all my attention. The pregnant part was really what had me all ears.

"Yes, son, I was just as shocked as you. I wanted to ask her if the baby was yours, but I didn't wanna overstep my bounds. I figured you would handle it when you saw her."

"Mom, Dad, can y'all please keep an eye on Nadia? I have to go find out if this baby is mine. If she tells me no, then I'll be back, and I won't bother Kyndall anymore. Just tell Nadia I had to go out of town on urgent business, and Luke, please don't tell Shawnee until I find out what's going on. Please help my parents look after Nadia and the baby."

"Bro, you know I got you. I'll tell her you want her at your parents' crib until you get back," Luke said. My mom didn't look too happy, but I looked at her with pleading eyes.

"Mama, please just do it for Junior and me." She rolled her eyes, but she kissed my cheek, and I headed out the door. Kyndall was going to make me kick her ass. She knew she was pregnant with my seed and didn't have the decency to tell me. I knew she was in her feelings, but this was some shit she needed her family by her side for. I hurried and got my private pilot on the line.

"Yo, Max, you busy, my man?"

"Nope, I'm on the strip, chillin'. What's good, my man?"

"I need you right now. I need to get to Memphis, like now."

"OK, what time will you be ready?"

"I'm ready right now. I'll be to you in like half an hour." I hung up, jumped in my whip and peeled off.

Kyndall

"Hey, boo, how are you feeling today?" Danni asked as she came into my room.

"I'm good, just tired as hell, and I feel fat as hell. I wasn't nearly this big with Nevaeh. I didn't get this far along, either, so I'm not going to complain." I was so excited, I just wish I had Cash here to enjoy this with me. I was going on seven months, and loving every moment of it.

"Girl, I'm so excited. Shawnee gon' have to share this baby with me." When she said that, I got sad as hell. I missed Shawnee so much. I knew I was going to have to call her soon because she would kill me if I had this baby without her. I was just scared she was going to tell Cash. It was not that I was trying to keep the baby from him, but I didn't need the stress he causes.

"So, when you gon' call yo' baby daddy?" she asked, causing me to roll my eyes. She had been on my ass about calling Cash, and that shit wasn't happening anytime soon.

"Soon." She gave me a smug look, but I didn't care. I was going to do this on my time, and she had to understand that. She didn't know Cash, and he was crazy. I knew once he found out, he was going to flip on my ass.

"I guess. I'm finna go to my boo's house so I will see you later. Call me if you need me." She kissed me on the jaw and headed out. Once she was gone, I grabbed my Kindle and found a book to read. I was so into the book I was reading, I didn't hear my phone ringing. When I saw that it was my Mom-Mom, I got excited.

"Hey, Mom," I answered.

"Hey, baby girl. How are you and my grandbaby doing?"

"We are doing good. I wish you could come down here and stay with me until I have the baby," I whined. I knew that would make her come. I just wanted some family here with me.

"So what would I tell Shawnee? You know she will have a fit because you didn't call her. With that being said, when are you going to call her? You know that girl misses you," she said, making me feel worse. I knew I should have called her, but I also knew she was going to tell Luke, and that was like telling Cash.

"I will call her, Mom-Mom. I promise."

"Good, after you do that, I will be on the first thing smoking. I have some questions for your doctor anyway, but I will call you later because my company just walked in."

"What company?" I asked just as she hung up. That lady thought she was slick.

Since I was home alone, I decided I would go and take a swim. I had been here all this time, and I hadn't touched the swimming pool. After I put my swimsuit on, I stood in the mirror and admired myself. Pregnancy looked good on me. I was headed to the pool, and I thought I heard a knock at the door, but I kept walking because no one really came over, and she had just left not too long ago. I knew it wasn't anyone for me, and she wasn't here, so I opened the door to the pool room and took a seat on the chair so I could pull my hair into a ponytail.

I was happy her pool was indoors because I didn't like to be outside. I slowly made my way to the pool and could have sworn I saw a shadow. I chopped it up to it being one of the trees. I grabbed a float once I was all the way in the pool and climbed on it. As soon as I thought I was on there good, the whole damn thing flipped over. I was pissed because I had fucked up my silk press. Shit, I had just gotten my damn hair done, and now I was going to have to go get this shit done over. I swam to the edge of the pool so I could get a towel. I had to use the bathroom anyway. I had eaten some pasta earlier, and apparently, my baby didn't like it.

"So, you really thought I wouldn't find you." As soon as I heard his voice, I shitted on my-damn-self. To make matters worse, I had on a thong. I was so embarrassed because my back was to him. I could smell him, and he wasn't even close to me. I stood there for a minute because I didn't want to face him.

"Kyndall, stop playing, with yo' shitty ass, and turn around and look at me." As much as I wanted to be mad, I couldn't help but laugh. I slowly turned around, and he was right there, looking good as ever. His dreads were neatly done, and he wore all black. I had to force myself not to lick my lips.

"Cash."

"Don't fucking Cash me, Kyndall." He had a scowl on his face, but that didn't take away from how sexy he was. "So you didn't think it was important for you to tell me you were having my baby?" he said as his eyes roamed my body. I felt naked under his eyes.

He made his way over to me, and my body froze. All he did was stare at my belly the whole time. He then grabbed my hand, signaling for me to follow him.

"Where is your bathroom?" he asked. I pointed in the direction of the bathroom, and we headed that way. Once we were in the bathroom, he sat me on the toilet, then cut the water on so I could take a shower. He went into the room, came back with some clothes for me to put on, then helped me in the shower. I was still stuck in the same spot. He turned me around so he could help me wash, and that was when the tears started rolling. I couldn't believe he had found me. Memphis was pretty big, so how in the hell did he know where to come? I wondered if Shawnee had ratted me out. I was going to kick her ass if she had.

He took his shirt off before picking me up and sitting me in the tub. Once I was comfortable, he sat on the toilet. He had his head in his hands, and I knew that meant he was trying to get his thoughts together.

"Cash," I called, and he lifted his head. Our eyes locked, and we just sat there for a minute. I guess he could read my mind because he took off the rest of his clothes and got in the tub with me. He held me as I cried. I knew deep down, he was mad at me for keeping this away from him.

"Do you still love me?" I asked. That was a crazy question, but I needed to hear him say it.

"If I didn't, I wouldn't be here. I should be asking you that. You're the one who hid from me and was going to have my baby and not tell me."

"It's not that I wasn't going to tell you, I just didn't want to get your hopes up. We all know having kids isn't my thing. I really didn't think I would make it this far. You know what happens every time I get pregnant."

"You know I would have been here every step of the way. Have I ever not been there when you needed me?" he asked as he washed my back. I felt nervous as hell. It was like it was my first time being around him.

"I know, it's just so hard for me. I didn't want to take you through that heartbreak," I said as I turned towards him. He kissed me, and my damn body felt like it melted. He stood up, helped me up and washed every inch of my body and that shit felt so good. Once he was done, he grabbed a towel and dried me off, then helped me put my clothes on. He helped me to bed, then he went back to shower. He put his gym shorts back on and climbed into the bed with me. He pulled me closer and wrapped his arms around me, cupping my stomach.

"What are we having?" he asked.

"I don't know. I really don't care as long as it's healthy." My baby was moving so damn much, I guess it knew its dad was here.

"I hope it's a girl," he said, causing me to smile. This felt perfect. I wish it could last forever, but I knew that wasn't going to happen.

"So when can I find out, because I wanna know."

"I actually go tomorrow. I have to go once a week. They did a procedure so the baby wouldn't come early."

"If I'm right, you will be seven months soon. Right?"

"Yep."

"OK. If it's cool with you, I wanna stay so I can go with you in the morning."

"I would love that. As long as you don't try and shoot me again." We both laughed. I knew he hadn't tried to shoot me, but I was still mad about it. He could have killed me. Shit, I wonder if he had killed Keem. I wondered how I could ask about Keem without making him mad. Hell, I kind of needed to know so I could collect my insurance money since that was all his ass was worth.

"Umm, is Keem dead?"

"Naw," was all he said. I left it at that because I really didn't care. For the rest of the night, we laid in bed and caught up on each other's lives. I had missed him so much.

Chapter Eighteen

Keem

I had been chilling for the past few weeks. The female I was fucking with had been keeping me high, and that was all I needed. I missed Chrissy, though. I had called her a few times, but she didn't answer, it made me wonder if she was dead. I pulled out my phone and called the hospital to see if she was there. When they told me she was, I got dressed so I could go see her. I needed her to know that soon as she was out of there, she needed to have her ass at my house.

The moment I walked into the hospital, I thought about my wife. I wondered if she was OK. I wished I could find her, that way I wouldn't need Chrissy. Hell, all I wanted was her anyway. I wondered if she would take me back. I didn't see why she wouldn't; hell, everyone makes mistakes. I was even willing to forgive her for fucking Cash.

Thinking of Cash, I hadn't seen him in a while. He had long ago stopped paying me, but I wish I had some money because I would get a lawyer. When he had hired me, we signed a contract, and it stated that he would have to pay me a lump sum if our partnership ever ended. I didn't think anything would happen, but I knew people outgrow each other. He trusted me, so he didn't even read over it.

I stopped at the desk to find out what room she was in, then headed to the elevator. As soon as I stepped off, I saw a fine-ass nurse. I guess she could feel me looking at her because she turned around and winked at me. I approached her and took the phone she was holding out her hand and locked my number in, then handed it back to her. No words needed to be spoken. I turned around and made my way to the room Chrissy was in.

Her eyes were closed, but they popped open when she heard my voice. "Where's my baby?" I asked.

"What are you doing here, Keem?"

"That's not answering my question, Chrissy."

"My baby died because of you, and I'm going to make sure you pay for that. Get the fuck away from me." She was yelling at that point, so I knew someone was going to come. Just as I was walking out the room, some nigga walked in.

"If it isn't the nigga I been looking for. You a hard nigga to find," he said as he put his hand on my shoulder.

"Nigga, get yo' hand off me." I jerked away from him. This nigga had me shook, but I wouldn't let him know that. "You don't want these problems. You fuck with me, you fuck with my brother, and we all know you don't want no smoke with Cash."

"Nigga, Cash don't fuck with you. We all know that. Be happy that we at this hospital because if we weren't, you would be dead. But don't worry, I'm going to see you sooner than you think, so make sure you say your prayers. I'm coming for you when you least expect it. You killed my son, so I'm going to kill you," was the last thing he said before his fist smashed into my face.

"Now get the fuck out," he said, stepping over me. I hurried my ass out of there. I knew at that point, I would have to leave the city. I tried my luck and called Kyndall's phone. When I got the message saying the number was disconnected, I threw my phone in the passenger seat.

I headed back to the hotel. I knew he wouldn't find me here, but I didn't want to take any chances. I grabbed all my shit and hit the road. I drove another hour outside of the city to a hotel. Once I was checked in, I laid down so I could get some sleep.

Nadia

"Hey, do you mind holding CJ while I shower?" I asked Cash's mom.

"He's my grandson, ain't he?" she barked. This lady was really getting on my nerves. She had been mean as hell from the moment I walked into her house. I couldn't wait until my six weeks were up so I could go to my own house.

I handed her CJ and walked out the room, headed straight to the shower. I was waiting for Cash to bring me something to eat. I was happy that he was back from his business trip because his mom was driving me crazy. She was strict as hell on what she let me eat, due to the fact that I was breastfeeding CJ.

After I was done with my shower, I went back to her room to get my baby. He was stretched out on her bed, looking just like Cash. I smiled before walking over to pick him up.

"Why would you wake him up? We all know you a sorry-ass mama, but you should know better than that. I will bring him to you when he wakes up. Now get out my room." It took everything for me not to curse her ass out, but I just walked out the room. Once I was outside the door, I let the tears roll. I went to the room I was staying in and called Nadeen.

"Hey, baby sis," she answered.

"Hey," I mumbled. I knew she would know I was crying.

"What's wrong?"

"I just don't think I can stay here. Can I just come home?" I was happy my sister and I were talking again. I missed her, and she was allowing me to build a relationship with my baby. I was so happy when I found out my sister had made sure she knew who I was.

"Yes, you can always come home, but you need to wait until your six weeks are up. I will bring Nya to stay with you for a few days while me and the hubby go on a mini-vacation, so check with Cash to be sure it's OK."

"OK, I will check with Cash soon as he gets here. He just got back on town today." We talked for a while longer, and I ended the call.

I had some homework I needed to get done, so I pulled out my laptop. Just as I was getting comfortable, Cash's mom walked into the room, holding my sweet baby. I wanted to roll my eyes, but I was too busy smiling.

"Hey, Mommy's baby," I said, grabbing my baby from her mean ass.

"Let me ask you something. What makes CJ different? Will you leave him like you left her?"

"Look, I'm going to tell you this only because I feel it will help you understand me. I was young when I had her. I begged my sister to let me get an abortion because I had gotten raped. I couldn't tell her that because I thought she wouldn't believe me. After I had her, I left because I didn't think I could be a good mother to her." By the time I was done talking, I was crying so hard.

"Ma, what are you doing to her?" I jumped because I didn't expect him to be here so soon.

"Nothing, now get this baby and get out," she said, picking CJ up and handing him to his dad. Once he was out the room, she looked at me with sad eyes. I was pissed because I wanted my damn food, but I knew that me and her needed to have this conversation.

"First thing I'm going to say is that I'm sorry. I shouldn't have judged you. Just know that everything will be OK. You will be a great mother when I'm done with you," she said, kissing me on the head. "Now go get yourself together and go get CJ before his daddy feeds him to death."

I just laughed because she wasn't lying. Cash thought because he cried, he was hungry. My baby was going to be fat as hell.

I went to the bathroom to clean my face, then headed to find Cash and CJ. I found them in the den, on the couch, knocked out. I wanted to get CJ, but I knew he was going to get mad. CJ didn't fuck with anybody when his daddy was around.

I had some clothes I needed to wash, so I went to do that. When I loaded the washer, I headed to fix my baby a bottle. I walked back in the den, and they were looking at the TV. It was funny because CJ looked like he was really into it.

"You gon' feed him, or you want me to feed him?"

"I will feed him. You good? What you and Mama was talking about?"

"Yea, I'm good. I wanted to see if you were OK with Nya staying with us for a while. Nadeen and her husband are going on a vacation."

"You don't have to ask me that, she's CJ's sister. Just let me know so we can get her room together." I wanted to jump for joy. I just knew he was going to say some crazy shit. I ran to the back and called my sister to tell her the good news, and she was just as happy as I was. When we ended the call, Cash stood at the door, looking good as always.

"I don't think I have ever seen you so happy about something. I want to question you, but I'm not because when you ready to tell me, you will. All I'm going to say is if you play with CJ like that, you won't live to talk about it. Now get this li'l nigga; he done threw up all over my damn shirt."

I jumped up and grabbed my baby. I missed him like he had been gone or something. I was kind of mad I had missed all these moments with Nya, but I couldn't wait to make it all up to her.

"I will be here for a few more days, so let me know what day you need to go and get Nya's room ready. I will take you to go get all the stuff, or you can just use my card to order what you need."

"OK, I will look at some stuff online today because she will be here next week. Nadeen said I could keep her for a week. You think Mrs. Lucille will come and help me with them?" I asked, and he just nodded his head.

"Go call her so she will know. I'm finna go to the pharmacy, then meet Luke. I will be back later," he said while kissing me on the forehead. He kissed CJ, then headed out the door. I was so happy that things were going well for us. I just knew it was going to be all bad.

Shawnee

"Baby, can you make some chicken!" Luke yelled from the living room. I hated when he did that. The living room was like three steps away, and he was yelling like I was upstairs.

"Yes, I can. Let me finish helping Joi read this book." It seemed he was eating more than me. Every time I turned around, he wanted something to eat, and each time, it was something particular.

"Daddy always hungry," Joi tried to whisper.

"I heard that," he yelled back. Joi and I burst out laughing. He swore Joi and I were always double-teaming him.

"It's OK, daddy, I like to eat, too." She had her head down, so she didn't notice he was standing right behind her. He picked her up and started tickling her. All I could do was laugh because she should have known that was coming.

"Stop playing in the kitchen, Luke. If you make my baby hit her head, I'ma kick yo' ass," I yelled, as he was getting closer to the end of the table. When I said that, he put her down and she ran out the kitchen.

I pulled out some chicken, then looked for some sides for us to eat. I was getting ready to clean the chicken when a FaceTime came through from a number I didn't know. I wiped my hand on a towel, then answered.

"Bitch, I wanna curse you out in so many ways, but I'm not. I'm just happy to see your face," I said as soon as Kyndall's face came on the screen.

"Girl, shut up. Yo' ass knew where I was. I just knew you were gon' come and get my ass," she laughed.

"I miss you so much, Kyndall. When are you coming home?" I asked. For some reason, I wanted to cry, but I had to shake that shit off fast. This baby was playing tricks on me, for real.

"I miss you, too, Shawnee. Hows Joi?" I noticed she avoided my question, but it was cool because I knew she would be back soon.

"Girl, she's doing good, but I have to show you something." I headed to the living room where my purse was. I pulled out the ultrasound and went back into the kitchen. Once I was in good lighting, I turned the camera around, and she let out a loud scream.

"Bitch, I'm about to be a godmama."

"Yassssss, but look at this." I looked at the camera and damn near choked on my own spit.

"Lukeeeeeee!" I yelled as I walked up the stairs. I had to let him see this shit for himself.

"What's up, baby?" he said, meeting me at the top of the stairs. I turned the phone so he could see Kyndall. Her stomach was big as hell.

"Yo, Cash gon' flip," I said.

"You might as well bring yo' ass home. How far along are you? Does Cash know? I can't wait till Mom-Mom sees you." She smiled, and that was all that mattered to me.

"Girl, stop asking all these damn questions. Shit, I can't answer one because you're asking another."

"Well, excuse me for being happy about seeing my cousin's face for the first time in months. Hell," I fussed. I had been checking on her, but there was nothing like seeing her or hearing her voice on my own.

"Now. I can't come until I have the baby. My doctor is here. She has me on bed rest until I give birth. I'm seven months, and yes, Cash knows."

"How the hell did he find out before me, and seven months? I'ma kick Danni's ass. She should have told me so I could have come and stayed with you. You needed your family." I had gotten sad because she shouldn't have gone through that alone. I was just happy she had made it past six months.

"I'm so happy for you and Luke. I know he's not ready for that nasty-ass attitude of yours," she joked.

"Girl, me too. I was scared at first, but I'm good now. I'm coming to see you. I will be there next week," I assured her. I had been waiting for this for months. I just wanted to hug her. I couldn't wait until I told Mom-Mom I had talked to her. I knew I had a dress I needed to finish, but my cousin was more important.

"I'm just happy Cash was happy. I think it's crazy that I will be giving him his first baby," she beamed. I looked at Luke, and he shook his head. I wanted to tell her the truth, but I had just gotten her back, and I wasn't willing to lose her again, not right now.

I talked over that comment. I caught her up on what was going on in my life, and she did the same. We stayed on the phone for hours. By the time we both hung up, it was three in the morning.

Chapter Nineteen

Luke

Thank God, Kyndall had resurfaced. I didn't know who was worse without her: Shawnee or Cash. They both better enjoy her because when she finds out Nadia and Cash have a baby, she was going to flip. I just prayed she didn't run away again.

The thing I was happy about was the fact that she was finally going to have a baby of her own. She deserved it. Cash was walking around like he was the man of the year. I was happy for my boy, though. He finally had the love of his life back. He had even gone as far as buying a new house so she would have a place of her own.

"Baby, can you help me take my bag downstairs?" I had to do a double take. She had three damn bags.

"Shawn, you only staying for a few days. Why do you need all of this?" I asked.

"One of them is stuff we got for the baby, and the other is shoes, and this one is clothes," she said, slinging the largest one.

"You could have just given her the baby stuff when she came home."

Shawnee was so damn extra. That was my baby, though, so I was all for it. On the way down the stairs, I peeked into Joi's room, and she was sleeping so peacefully. I wanted to wake her up because I knew if she woke up and Shawnee was gone, she was going to have a fit.

As soon as I made it downstairs, my business phone rang. I looked, and it was one of the niggas who worked for me named Keys. Once I had the bags by the door, I picked up.

"What's good?"

"Nothing much, just checking in, boss man. I just did the pickup. I'm getting ready to leave the warehouse now. I just texted you the numbers."

"OK, cool. You can take the rest of the day off so you can spend some time with ya girl." I knew his girl was in the hospital and that they had just lost a baby. I saw Cash go through that shit, so I knew how it could affect a person.

"Thanks," was all he said before ending the call.

I looked, and Joi was at the top of the stairs, rubbing her eyes. I smiled and held my arms out to her. As always, she ran to me. As soon as I picked her up, she laid her head on my shoulder, and before I knew it, she was knocked out. I laid her on the couch and headed back to the room so I could get some pussy before dropping them off.

****

Later that night...

I had so much I needed to get done while Shawnee was gone and while I didn't have Joi. I knew she was going to want to come home tomorrow. She didn't like being away from home.

My phone had been ringing all damn day, but I hadn't answered because it was someone calling from an unknown number. I was tired of them calling, so I decided to answer.

"Yea?"

"Luke," Meia whined on the phone.

"What the fuck do you want? And why the fuck you calling me back to back like that?"

"I wanted to pick Joi up and spend some time with her." I had to laugh. Did this bitch really think I would allow her near Joi?

"Meia, get off my line."

"Either you can let me see her, or the police gon' be knocking at your door." When she said that, I wished I could jump through the damn phone. She had lost her fucking mind. She knew not to play with me like that.

"Meia, play if you want. You know you don't want to go to war with me."

"Fuck you. Yo' days are short anyway, bitch," was all she said before hanging up. I pulled the phone from my ear and looked at it like she was still on it. I made a mental note to have one of my niggas go find her blow head ass.

I headed to the warehouse so I could meet Cash. When I pulled up, I called Shawnee to see what she was doing. I missed my baby like crazy, and she had only been gone for a few hours.

"Hey, baby," she answered.

"Hey. What y'all doing?" I asked.

"Nothing, finna cook something to eat. Baby, Kyndall is so big, you would think she was having twins. I'm so happy for her, baby."

"Me too, baby. Guess who just called me."

"I hope you not finna say Meia."

"Yep. She asked if I could let her get Joi, then when I told her no, she gon' tell me that she was going to the police. I've been trying to let that blow brain ass bitch be great, but she is pushing me."

"Fuck that bitch. She better stay in her lane. That hoe knows better. Let her hang herself, baby." Shawanee was my medium. When I had a bad day and wanted to kill everyone walking, she always helped me clear my head and get shit together.After we talked for a while longer, Cash pulled up, and we headed to the warehouse.

 I could tell he had something on his mind, but I wanted to wait until we were alone before I asked him what was wrong. He spoke to everyone, then walked into his office.

"What's on ya mind?" I asked as soon as the door closed behind me.

"I'm torn. I love Kyndall, but I can't just leave Nadia and my son. That was one of the reasons I didn't push Kyndall to come back. As long as they are in different cities, I feel like I can keep shit together, but I know that after Shawnee comes back, Kyndall will be ready to come home. I just don't want to lose her again. I know she is going to flip when she finds out about CJ. Hell, I know Nadia gon' flip when she finds out I've been going to see Kyndall. Then, to top all that, Kyndall thinks she's giving me my first child.

That shit gon' kill her. I don't see how niggas live double lives. This shit got a nigga tired as hell."

"That's why my ass sticking with Shawnee. But you gon' have to figure out something because the shit's going to hit the fan. You know Shawnee Team Kyndall all day. She has been keeping yo' secret, but that's not gon' last long."

Cash was playing with fire. He knew the day he went to Memphis, he should have told Kyndall. Shawn had been cool about it, but I knew she was going to have to tell Kyndall at some point.

"Let's go handle these niggas so I can get home to my son." I nodded and followed him out the office.

I looked around and admired the team we had built. When we lost Dre, we promoted Keys, and he had been doing well. We almost never had issues with his team, and most times, he handled it before we could.

"So, what's good? Give me some good news, Keys," Cash said as he took his seat next to me.

"We up ten percent this week alone. Money is flowing, and pill poppers are getting high." Cash let out a chuckle, and so did I. Keys was a jokester, but he took care of business, and that was all that mattered to me. He was nothing like Dre. Dre was a slacker. Hell, Keys had just lost a baby, and that nigga had been grinding through it all. The rest of them gave us an update, then we all headed out. All I wanted to do was get some much-needed sleep.

Meia

"Tory, you are fucking me too hard!" I yelled. He had been taking lines back to back all day, and that shit was killing me. He was mad at Keys because he wouldn't let him borrow money. He had changed the most in two weeks. Like, this nigga was a whole new person. Just a week ago, he treated me like a queen; now he had me out here selling my pussy like I was a two-dollar hoe.

"Shut up before you fuck up my nut," he yelled back while yanking my hair. I knew he had to have a handful of my hair when he stopped.

I was so happy when he nutted. I grabbed my shit and went out the door. I was dry, so there was no reason to wipe myself off, and my shit burned like a motherfucker. It felt like someone had stuck a firecracker in my pussy, or like I had sniffed a line with my pussy. Y'all know what I mean. Hell, that shit hurt.

"Don't come back without a plan, either!" he yelled as I ran out the door. Everything in me wanted to say fuck it and never come back here, but I knew he would find me, just like I knew Luke would. I was so fed up and frustrated.

I jumped in my car and headed to my house. I hadn't been there in a while because I didn't want Tory to know I still had it. Hell, he would try and sell the motherfucker just to get high. I was fucked up, but not like him. Once I made it home, I headed to the shower. I needed to think of a way to get Joi. I wouldn't let Tory hurt her, I just wanted to get some money out of Luke so Tory would leave me the fuck alone.

The whole time I was in the shower, I was trying to think of a way to get her. I had tried the thing with his mom, but she wasn't going for it. She told me she couldn't go behind Luke's back like that. Joi wasn't in school, and I knew he wouldn't just let me come get her.

"Fuck, how can I pull this off?" I yelled. After I got out the shower, I called my mom to see if she would get her.

"Mom, I wanna see my baby," I fake cried.

"Don't call me with that bullshit. The last time I helped you, Luke wouldn't let me see her for a whole year, so whatever you got going on, leave me out of it," she said before hanging up in my face. I wanted to scream. I had to think of something. My last resort was calling Luke, but I guess it wouldn't hurt to try.

I called him, and he shut that shit down fast. I laid on my floor for hours, mad at myself for talking so much. I had heard him tell Keys he had a way for them to get some extra money, so I knew I couldn't return without Joi.

I needed to get high; that was the only way I would be able to think. I got up and went to find my purse. I couldn't think of where I had thrown it when I had come into the house. I always kept a little blow in my compact mirror for when he was acting funny with his shit. I was happy as hell when I opened the compact mirror and saw that I had enough for three lines. I took the first line, and my mind started rolling. I jumped in my car and headed to Luke's mom's house. It was the weekend, so I knew she would be there with her.

It was late night, so I knew my plan was going to work. I pulled into her driveway after I cut my lights off. I thought about parking down the street, but I didn't want to take a chance on someone hearing Joi yell. That baby knows she could wake up a whole neighborhood.

Since I knew Joi was probably in her room, I went to the back of the house. Luke's mom made his old room Joi's room. One thing I knew about that room was that the window didn't lock.

"So, you were gonna just handle this without my help?" Tory barked, scaring the shit out of me. I looked around, trying to figure out where the hell his ass had come from.

"Tory, what are you doing here?" I whispered.

"I pulled up to ya crib and was gonna scare the shit out of you, but when I saw you coming out, I decided to follow you." I was so fucking annoyed. I did not want him doing this with me, but since he was here, I figured we'd better hurry up and get this done. I went to the bathroom window and prayed I could fit through it. I knew I wouldn't be able to get out of it so I would have to use her bedroom window to exit.

"Why you looking confused? Ya little crackhead ass can fit in that window. When you get in, let me in through another window." I rolled my eyes and sucked my teeth.

"Tory, why can't you just wait in the car?"

"Meia, I ain't waiting in no damn car. Plus, this is Luke's mama's house, so there's probably so much shit in here we can take."

"Tory, I am not robbing his mother. That was not in the plan." He pulled his gun out and placed it at the center of my back.

"You gon' do what the fuck I say, or all three of y'all will die tonight."

"OK, meet me at the next window so I can let you in," I said a little under a whisper. The bathroom window was unlocked. I slid in, praying no one was on the toilet when I opened the curtains. The bathroom door was open, and I could see the light from the TV in the den. I then ran to the room that was next to the bathroom, which was Luke's mom's room, and she wasn't in there, so I assumed she had fallen asleep in the den, as usual. Once I made sure everything was clear, I opened the window for Tory. It was a good thing Luke's mom was still in the den sleeping because if not, this wouldn't be easy. After double checking she was still asleep, I headed to the room Joi was in with Tory trailing close behind me.

"Meia, is that you?" I heard Luke's mom's voice. *FUCK!* I thought she was sleeping.

"Mama, please just go lay back down. I decided to come get Joi for a couple of days."

"Meia, Luke didn't tell me anything like that, and who is this man you got in my house? How the fuck did y'all get in here?"

"Listen, lady, go the fuck back in that room where you were, and mind ya damn business."

"Nigga, that's my granddaughter, and she is my business." Tory pulled his gun out, and my eyes grew big as shit.

"Tory, what the fuck are you doing?"

"Meia, shut the fuck up and go get in the car."

"No, I will not leave and let you hurt her."

"You will do what I said, or I will kill ya daughter, then her, and let you live." He didn't have to tell me twice. I headed straight to the door, but before I left, I begged him not to kill her.

"If I hear that car peel off, she's as good as dead. Now go wait for me like I told you to." The minute I stepped on the step, I heard, *pop, pop.* The tears rolled down my face instantly, and all I could think was, *What did I get myself into?* I hurried and ran to the car before Joi woke up. My baby must have been tired because she was out, and hadn't woken up yet. I was in the car, crying my heart out. The car door opened, and Tory jumped in with Luke's mom's purse and some of her jewelry.

"Did you kill her, Tory?"

"No, the bitch will live. She was doing too much slick talking, so I smacked her ass around a little."

"Tory, I heard gunshots."
 "She'll be OK!" he snapped, and started the car up and peeled off.

"Tory, we weren't supposed to do that. Luke is going to go crazy."

"FUCK LUKE! I'm so fucking tired of hearing about him."

"I have to call him and tell him to get to his mama to get her some help."

"If you call him, I'm going to kill you and your daughter, now fuck with me if you want to."

I sat in the car and continued to cry my heart out. I had to figure out a way to call Luke to get to his mama.

Luke

The house was so fucking peaceful, but I missed Shawnee and Joi. I hoped Shawnee came home asap. I wanted to call her and tell her ass that I was sick so she could come home. I got out of bed and showered. I knew what I was going to put on, so that took no time.

I was cleaned up and ready to run the streets. When I got in the car, I called Keys so I could see what was up with him.

"What's good, boss man?" he joked. He knew I didn't like that shit, and that was why he did it.

"Shit, just checking. Where ya at?" I asked as I pulled out of my driveway.

"At the warehouse. Me and Cash just pulled up," he advised me. I was digging his work ethic. He was all about the money, up bright and early every day.

"OK. Cool, I'm headed that way," I told him before ending the call. I rolled a blunt while I was on the way since I hadn't had one before my shower. I got there in no time since I didn't live far. Keys was in the warehouse, giving orders, and Cash was in his office, so I headed in there with him.

"Shit, Keys keep moving like this, nigga, and we can retire asap," I laughed as I closed the door to his office.

"Damn right. I think I'm going to promote him again," Cash said as he ran money through the money machine. "Shit, sales been going up, and we don't have to deal with the little niggas. Hell, how did we skip over him and choose Dre?"

"I don't know, but what's done is done," I added. I lit the blunt and took a seat. I was sitting so I could see Keys talking to the workers. Cash cut on the PA system so we could hear what was going on.

"I miss my wife, nigga. Kyndall gon' have to bring her ass home 'cause I don't think I can take her being gone like that." I was fussing like a bitch. I didn't care, though. Hell, I wanted my baby home with me. A nigga was hungry as hell. Shit, she had breakfast ready every morning, and I missed that shit.

"Shit, I miss Kyndall, too, but I need to get shit in order first. Hell, I gotta at least get Nadia out my mom's house first."

"Kyndall gon' kill yo' ass."

"Who you telling? You know Moms fucks with Kyndall the long way, so I know that little relationship she done built with Nadia gon' go right out the window. Hell, you know all y'all Team Kyndall, so Nadia has no chance."

Once he was done counting the money, I closed the blinds so he could put it in the safe. No one knew where the safe was but he and I. Honestly, it was in plain sight, but that smart-ass nigga had found a way to hide it.

"Call Keys in here. I don't know about you, but I wanna lay under my girl." I was all for that. I jumped up and opened the door fast as hell.

"Yo, Keys. Come let us holla at ya," I yelled. He set the bag down he was holding and headed towards us. When we walked in, Cash gestured for him to sit down. I went and stood by Cash.

"I just want to let you know that we see you working and we appreciate that shit. I got an opportunity for you if you open to it," Cash said as he sat on the edge of his desk.

"Y'all know I'm ready for whatever. I just wanna get some money so I can take care of my family."

"By the way, how is your girl doing?" I asked.

"She's OK, just taking it one day at a time. Shit, I'm ready for her to get well so I can put another baby in her," he joked.

"OK, so we need to head out of town for a day or two. Do you think you can hold shit down while we're gone?" His eyes lit up.

"Yea, I got y'all. I've been waiting for a chance to prove myself."

"Good, the only thing is, I don't want that nigga you be with around my shit. I trust you, Keys, and that's not normal. Show me you can handle shit, and we can talk about a promotion," Cash added. We talked about a few more things, then we headed out.

I went home to pack a small bag, and Cash did the same. Within an hour, we were headed to the airstrip. I couldn't wait to see my baby's face. My dick was getting hard just thinking about her ass.

■■

Three Hours Later...

"Nigga, wake up, we here," Cash said, shaking my shoulder.

"Damn, nigga, you didn't have to shake a nigga like that. What, are you trying to give me shaken baby syndrome or some shit? I'm going to have to watch CJ around yo' ass," I fussed as I got up.

"Really?"

"Fuck you mean, really? Hell yea. You gon' have a nigga head hurting doing that shit. Wait till I tell Shawnee."

"Go ahead. I'll just tell her yo' ass was dreaming about a female, and you were calling her name in yo' sleep, so who will she be madder at?" he spat, grabbing his duffle.

"So we going that low? I'll just tell Kyndall about Nadia, then we'll see who mad." He stopped walking and gave me an evil-ass look, and I burst out laughing. This nigga looked like he was going to cry.

"Fuck you," was all he said before walking off as I laughed my ass off. I grabbed my bag and followed him to a waiting SUV.

"We need to stop and get them something to eat. Ain't no way we can pop up on two pregnant females with no food, that's like a death threat. I don't know about you, but I wanna live," I told him as we pulled off from the airport lot. He told the driver to stop at The Cheesecake Factory, then pulled a blunt out of the console.

"My nigga," I joked. Cash always knew what a nigga needed. There was no feeling like waking up to a fat-ass blunt.

While he lit the blunt, I called and ordered their food so it would be ready when we got there. Thirty minutes later, we pulled up to the house they were living in, and I was amazed. That motherfucker was huge.

"Damn, homegirl living good. I think this motherfucker might be bigger than mine."

"Hell naw, nigga, yo' shit the size of a small island," he said while laughing. He wasn't lying, though. My shit was huge.

As soon as the truck stopped, we jumped out and headed towards the door. Cash knocked, and their homegirl answered.

"Hey, Danni! What's going on, crazy? Where's Kyndall?" Cash asked while pulling baby girl in for a hug. I guessed they had heard his voice, so they both ran to the door. The minute we got in the house, Shawnee jumped in my arms, and Kyndall pulled Cash in for a hug and kiss.

"I missed you so much, Luke."

"I missed ya sexy ass, too." I kissed her forehead, nose, then lips. The minute we were getting into a heated lip-locking session, my phone rang. The number was unknown, but I still picked up in case it was a work issue.

"Yo, who this?"

"Luke, Mama is hurt. You have to go check on her right now!" Meia screamed through the phone.

"What the fuck you talking about, Meia?" I barked into the phone, but all I heard was a dial tone. I didn't know what was going on, but if something had happened to my mama, where the fuck was my baby?

To be continued…

CPSIA information can be obtained
at www.ICGtesting.com
Printed in the USA
LVHW041948061120
670968LV00003B/417